THE SWAN QUEEN

Niall Jills

contents

CHAPTER 1

"Emma can you come zip me up dear?" Regina asks me.

"Sure babe." I say. "Can you do me a favor and button up one more button at the top.. I can see your black lace bra." I say and she chuckles at me. "I'm serious babe.. My dick got hard.. And if I get turned on by seeing you like that and I've already seen you naked.. Then I know that others are turned on as well and haven't seen you naked."

"Yes dear."

"Thank you babe.. I really don't want everyone to see what's only for me to see." I smack her ass and she smiles at me. "Mmmm.. Nice ass Madam Mayor." I walk away to head down stairs and get the kids some breakfast before school..

"You are such a little bitch you know that!" Henry says to his sister.

"HENRY DANIEL SWAN-MILLS!" I yell.

"Ma I'm so sorry."

"Don't apologize to me.. Apologize to your sister."

"I'm sorry Sam."

"Henry go tell your mother I'm taking Sam to the bus stop and you're riding with us."

"Yes ma'am."

"Thank you.. Sam baby let's go."

"What about breakfast mom? I have a test and I need a fresh mind."

"I'll get you something on he way."

"Pancakes and cookies for snacks?"

"You better not tell your mother.. She would kill me."

"Deal." She says and I take her to get breakfast and to the bus stop.

Knock Knock

"Mom are you dressed?" Henry asks.

"Yes my handsome boy."

"Good morning.. Ma said she's taking Sam to the bus stop and I'm riding with you guys today."

"Why? What's wrong?"

"I said something bad."

"What did you say?"

"Sam is always in my business.. You know she told Violet that I was a player."

"(Laughs) Henry you're too young for this."

"Mom I'm fifteen and a half.. I have feelings for her and we.."

"Do me and your ma need to talk to you again?"

"Eww!! God no.. I know what I'm doing.. I just need Sam to stay out of my business."

"And what are you planning on doing Mr.?"

"Mom you're missing the point."

"Baby you ready?" I yell upstairs.

"Coming."

"Without me? Now that's not fair?" I say.

"Gross!!" Henry yells.

"Our son is here dear."

"I'm well aware.. Henry come eat your breakfast." I say and he comes down the stairs with Regina. "My God you're beautiful." I smile at Regina.

"Not so bad yourself Sheriff Swan-Mills." She says and we all walk to the car.

"Thank you."

"You're welcome.. So why do Henry have to ride with us?"

"Because he said something very disturbing to his sister and I didn't like it."

"Oh he told me that she told a very special young lady his secret."

"Oh so he told you he called Samantha a bitch? Or was it something like.. 'Youre such a little Bitch', I think that's what it was.. Yeah."

"HENRY DANIEL SWAN-MILLS!"

"Mom I'm sorry, but she.."

"No buts.. You don't talk to your sister that way.. Infact you don't talk to any woman that way.. We raised you better than that."

"I know and I'm sorry."

"You're grouned for the rest of the week." My wife says.

"Mom Jake party is Friday."

"And you should have thought about that before you called your sister a little bitch."

"That's not fair.. Did she tell you guys that she's.."

"No sir don't try and get her in trouble because you got caught." Regina cuts him off.

"Your mother is right." I say pulling up the the school.

"Fine. Bye."

"Excuse me are you forgetting something?" I ask.

"I love you guys."

"Love you to kid." I say.

"Bye." He says shutting the door.

"Emma?" Regina says.

"Yeah baby?"

"Can you take the high way today on the way to work?"

"Sure thing babe." I look over at my beautiful wife and she's checking her emails on her phone.. I wonder why she wanted to take the long way today and it's Monday and the traffic is bad today because of the voting. "Hey babe?"

"Yes dear?" She answers but not even looking at me.

"Why did you want to take the long way today?"

"I just wanted to enjoy some extra time with my wife."

"Mmmm.. Thanks sweet if you baby." I smile at her and she takes her seat belt off.

"Ugh babe.. You might want to put that seat belt back on."

"And you my dear, might want to watch the rode." She smiles as she reaches over to undo my pants.

"(Gasps) Gina baby."

"Relax baby." I can't believe my wife is stroking me while I'm driving. What is I run into a fucking tree or someone's car? What if I hit someone?"Emma, you know I love you right?"

"Yes baby.. I love you too but you don't have to do that." She continues her teasing strokes and before I could even think she is already going for it.. "Gina.. Baby (Gasps) (Moans) Fuck!" Her tongue feels so good. I love it when she teases me with that tongue.. She starts off with nice long licks. I feel her other hand squeezing my balls. "Fuck Regina!" I have a very tight grip on the stirring wheel.

"I missed you daddy." She takes me in her mouth and I couldn't help but look down at her and watch her head move up and down. "You better be watch the road." She says.

"(Moans) Yes ma'am." I can't believe she's doing this while I'm driving.. "Right there baby.. Just like that." I grab a hold to her hair as she moves up and down on me very slowly.. "That's it baby." She going faster this time.. "Oh baby.. Deep throat me and swallow my load in your mouth Madam Mayor." I say and takes me all the way in your mouth and squeeze my balls.. That did it for me.. I exploded in her mouth. "Fuck!" I cam so hard.. I held myself in her mouth until I was down cuming.

"Mmmm.. I love it when your warm cum go down my throat."

"(Panting) What the fuck was that about Regina?"

"I'm sorry, I thought you was going to like it dear?" She looks in the mirror and wipe her mouth and fix her hair.

"Oh I loved it.. I just wasn't expecting it."

"I know.. That's why I did it."

"(Panting) Should I pull over and let you drive so I can repay the favor?" I ask.

"No.. I'm not ruining my last pair of panties." She says taking out some panties from her purse.

"Damn.. So you're prepared?"

"Yes my love." When we stop at the red light she takes off her panties and puts the clean pair on.

"You are a very dirty woman Madam Mayor."

"Only for you." She smiles at me.

"Thank you baby."

"You're welcome." And we are at her building.. "And Emma dear?"

"Yes my love?"

"Put these in the inside of your suit pocket." She puts the underwear that she just took off inside my pocket. "Sorry if there a little to wet.. I couldn't help myself." She then walks off into the crowd.

"Madam Mayor I have a question." One of the reporters says.

"An I might have an answer." My wife responds as she looks at me and smile.. I smile back and drive off.

CHAPTER 2

"Good afternoon baby." I say kissing my wife.

"Hello dear."

"How was work?"

"Very stressful. And you?"

"Mine was good, but I'll give you a stress reliever before you close those beautiful eyes tonight."

"And I'm sure you.."

"What's your stress reliever mom?" Henry asks.

"Thinking about putting another baby in your mom tonight." I say.

"EMMA!" Regina yells.

"That's gross mom."

"You asked Kid."

"Well you could have lied."

"I don't lie to my children.. SAMANTHA!" I yell upstairs.

"She's not here yet." Henry says.

"Where did she go.. She was outside before I got in the shower." I say.

"Ryan showed up and she said they were going to the store."

"She left with a boy?" Regina asked.

"Yes ma'am." Henry says with a smile.

"You like getting her trouble don't you kid?"

"She should stay out if my shit.. Business.. I meant business.. Then I wouldn't mind helping her out.. She helped me.. I help her.. It's simple."

"Henry if you swear one more time, I'm going to have to leave the Mayor's Office."

"Sorry mom.. Sam just.. Nothing."

"So lying to your parents is simple?" I ask and he just looks at me and then back at Regina who has an eyebrow raised.

"No.. Ma it's not like that."

"Call her and tell her that I said to get back here right this minute." My wife said with attitude in her voice.

"Ugh.. Yes.. Yes ma'am." Henry goes to the other room and call her.

"You're sexy when you mad."

"Mrs. Swan?" My wife warns me.

"To you that's Mrs. Swan-Mills.. Or should I remind you?" I now have my hands around her waist from behind. "You smell good."

"No I don't.. I've been working all day."

"Mmmm.. I know you have.. But you do smell loving.. Mmmmm.."

"Now is not the time for that." She says reaching in the cabinets.

"Time for what baby?" My eyes are only focused on her ass.. Mmmm..

"I can feel you behind me.."

"Damn that ass.. Baby let's order take out and skip on cooking."

"Not a chance."

"Mmmm.. But I want you so bad." I whisper in her ear with a little bite on the neck.

"(Gasps) Mmmm.. Do you now?" She asks and she brushes her ass against my front. Fuck!!

"(Moans) Yes." I say grabbing it and giving it a little squeeze.

"Then you're going to have to wait.. Sorry Daddy."

"Mmmm.. Fuck!! Gina baby."

"She said she'll be here soon." Henry walks in and say.

"Thanks kid." I say reaching for a chair to sit down.. Fuck!! Why does my wife tease me? How am I going to sit here like this?

"Welcome?" Henry says.

"Emma you okay dear?" Regina ask as she puts the lasagna in the oven. No I'm not fine Gina.. I'm horny and I'm standing straight up..

"Fine babe.. Fine."

"You sure?" She asks with a smirk.

"Screw you." I smile at her.. "I'm.. I have to go to the bathroom." I say getting up.

"Can you hold it until dinner is ready?" She asks.

"Funny.. I was trying to get you to hold it five minutes ago."

"You to need therapy." Henry says.

"What I need is to go to the bathroom.. Excuse me." I say walking away." And Regina just laughs..

"Hurry up Emma." Gina says.

"Yes MadamMayor." I say once the door is closed.. FUCK!! "Mm mmm.." I jerk off thinking about my beautiful sexy wife.. "(Moans) Shit!!"

"Open the door." Regina says on the other side..

Shit!!!

"Gina not now baby.. Ah!!"

"Okay." She says and somehow she just walks in..

"Fuck Gina!" I yell.

"Keep your voice." She closes the door and locks it.. But I don't stop.. I keep going and she just looks at me smiling. "You're so sexy." She says.

"(Moans) Gina.. Mmmm.. Get out." I say.

"Mmmm.. I dont think so." She walks toward me and get on her knees. "Stop." She says and she moves my hands.

"Get up Gina.. You don't have to do that.. Im.. (Gasps)." Her mouth is so soft and warm.. And it doesn't help because I was already close..

"(Moans) Fuck!" I hold her hair back and look down at her.. She's looking me dead in the eyes as she takes me. "I'm about to cum Gina."

"Mmmm.." She hums to tell me to going ahead and I do as I'm told..

"Ah!!! Mmmm.. (Panting) Gina.. I love you."

"I love you too dear.. Now come on.. Dinner is almost ready and Samantha is here." She says getting up to clean her mouth and brush her teeth.

"(Panting) I.. I'm.."

"Cat got your tongue dear?" She asks.. No, but your beauty did..

"Just looking at my wife."

"You can look at me later.. I have to feed our children dinner.."

"Will you feed ne after?" I ask smirking.

"Depends."

"On what?" I ask.

"How you behave at dinner of course."

"And do you want me to behave?" I whisper in her ear from behind.
"Good or bad? Naughty or Nice?"

"Surprise me." She smiles and she walks toward the door, but before she leaves I smack her ass.. HARD!! "AH!!! Emma!"

"That's right.. Same my name baby."

"(Laughs) You're such a child."

"Why are you two in the bathroom together." Sam asks.

"Don't ask.. Just forget a out it." Henry says.

"Fine with me?"

"Good choice baby." I say.

"Mom your lips stick is.. You know.." Henry says to Regina and I just laughs.

"Well if someone wasn't so messy then maybe my lip stick would have been just fine." Regina says looking at me.

"Wow.. So it's my fault?" I ask.

"You made the mess.. I just cleaned it up."

"Eww!! You two are gross.. I'm eating in my room tonight." Henry says.

"No sir you will not.. We are eating as a family.. Like always."

"Then can we talk as a family? And I'm just gone say you too were kissing and ma messed it up." He says.

"(Laughs) Of course.. Emma dear can you help set the table?"

"Sure babe." I getting up off the couch..

CHAPTER 3

"*(Laughs) Damn.*" I whispers.

"What's so funny dear?" Regina asks.

"Nothing.. Just reading a message."

"From who? You seem pretty into that message."

"Oh it's no one.. I cooked breakfast when I got back from my morning run.. (Laughs)."

"I have seem to have lost my appetite." She walks off mad.

"What's your problem?" I ask.

"Nothing Emma.. Good morning to you as well and yes I slept fine.. I will be home around 5pm this afternoon.. No I don't need lunch today.. And yes, you are taking the kids to school.. Since you didn't ask me this morning, I figured I could just say it all for you.. Have a nice day.." She then walks out the door.

What the Fuck!!

"REGINA!" I yell.

"What Emma!?"

"Lose the fucking attitude.. What's wrong with you?"

"I told you nothing.. Now drop it."

"You drop it."

"I'm not arguing with you.. I'm going to work." She says and my phone bings.. It's a text message. "(Laughs) Crazy as hell." I say.

"You know what? Forget." Regina says walking to her car.

"Regina!" I yell again.

"Leave me alone Miss Swan.. Keep talking to your whore." She says.

"What tha fuck are you talking about?"

"Bye Emma."

"Bye Regina.. And stop with the Miss Swan shit!"

"Whatever Miss Swan!" She yells before driving off.

"Fuck!!" I yell.

Later That Day....

"Hey Danielle can you pick up the paper from the front and fill it out please. I have a meeting coming up?"

"I can't I have to go."

"Your shift started an hour ago."

"Mayor Swan-Mills has asked to see me." She says.

"What does Regina want with you?"

"I don't know boss.. All o know is when you go see her you don't come back with a job."

"I'll call her right now.. You don't have to go over there."

"No! Boss it's okay, I'm sure your wife just wants to have a normal conversation."

"Regina knows I'm short handed today and she called you over there."

"I'm sorry.. I'll try my best to be back as fast as I can."

"It's fine.. Take your time."

"Thank you." She says walking out the door.

Regina's Office..

"Good morning Madam Mayor." Danielle says.

"Morning.. Have a seat."

"Yes ma'am.. What can I do for you?"

"Are you sleeping with my wife?"

"Excuse me?"

"Emma.. My wife.... Are you two sleeping together?"

"I don't know where you got your information or what stunt you are trying to prove but.."

"And you still haven't answered my question."

"No."

"No you haven't answered my question or no you're not fucking my wife?"

"I'm not sleeping with Emma."

"You two have seem to be getting very close."

"We just work together.. That's it "

"You sure do text alot."

"Yeah.. Work stuff."

"Work stuff? Right.. How was your night? Mine was pretty boring?"

"Excuse me?"

"Just reading you and Emma's messages."

"Mayor Mills.. I mean Swan-Mills.. Sorry.. Me and Emma are friends okay.. That's it."

"Morning run? Would you like to join me? Or maybe the last message you said.. What was it let me find it.. Oh here it is.. I had a great time and I can't wait to do it again."

"Madam Mayor we went for a run ND that's it I swear.. We.."

"ENOUGH!!" Regina yells.

"Tell me Madam Mayor, Have you talked to your WIFE about this?"

"That's none of your business."

"Asking me who I'm fucking is none of your business." Danielle then gets up and walks to the door.

"I have ever right to ask you if it has something to do with my wife."

"Yeah.. Well you keep saying wife like you're trying to prove something.. It's like you're afraid she's going to leave you.. Or someone with take her away from you."

"Watch it."

"Regina of you do your job right, then Em-ma has no reason to leave you."

"Do my job right? What does that mean?"

"Whatever you want it to mean.. It was nice talking to you Madam Mayor.. Have a nice day.. I mean that is what you told Emma this morning wasn't it? (Laughs)." Danielle then walks out the door.

Back At The Station..

"Hey what did she say?" I ask Dani.

"Nothing.. I'll have that paper work done in a few minutes."

"Dani what did she say?"

"Are you cheating on your wife?"

"Excuse me?"

"We'll she thinks that you are and she accused me of fucking you."

"Are you serious?"

"She thinks you're sleeping around with somebody.. And oh yeah.. She has all of our messages."

"How did she even.. Of course.. She switched our phone plan.. Now she gets all of my messages."

"Well I did piss her off."

"What did you do?"

"I told her that she should talk to you about it and I left."

"You know what? Forget the paper work.. It's for her anyway.. She'll just have to wait on it.. I'm leaving early.. When Graham gets here tell him I told you to go home.. Graham and Killian come stay for the overnight shift.."

"Thanks boss.. See you in the morning.."

"Goodnight Dani."

"Goodnight."

Later That Night At Home...

"Hey mom." Henry says.

"Hey kid.. Where's your sister?"

"Behind you."

"Hey mom." Samantha says.

"Hey baby.. Listen, how about you two go and get dinner.. I don't care what you pick.. Eat out and bring me and your mother something."

"But ma already started cooking." Henry says.

"Yeah.. She's not going to finish.. We need to talk."

"Right.. I'm driving." Sam says.

"Be careful." I say before going I'm the kitchen.

"Yes mom." Sam says before they leave.

"What the hell is your problem?" I ask Regina when I go into the kitchen but she doesn't answer me. "ANSWER ME!" I yell.

"Come down dear.. I'm not in the mood for your shit."

"My shit?"

"Yes." She then turns off the oven and stove.. She knows she's not going to finish.

"We'll get in the mood because we're having this conversation."

"Not I'm not."

"The hell you are.. What's wrong with you? And why in the hell did you accuse Dani of sleeping with me?"

"Oh so you have nicknames for each other? Do you call her that when you're fucking her?"

"Regina stop it."

"Did you tell her to stop? I mean she did inform me that if I didn't do my job right then you'll leave me.. Was she right? Did you get tired of me?"

"You're acting crazy.. You know damn well I'm not fucking her.. And no, you do your job just fine.."

"(Laughs) Whatever."

"Regina why are you acting like this? We we're fine yesterday."

"Things change.. Or should I say people change.. Do you fuck her as good as you fuck me? Or do you fuck her better?"

"Stop saying that shit!!! I'm not fucking nobody but you."

"Doesn't feel like it."

"You wasn't complaining before."

"That was before I found out you we're fucking that bitch."

"You know what? Believe what you want to believe."

"So it's true then? You're fucking that whore and I'm not good enough for you you.. Does she have any kids?"

"What does that have to do with anything?"

"We'll maybe you think she's tighter than I am.. You know.. Considering I.."

"Don't you dare finish that sentence.. You body is perfectly fine the way it is.. It's the same as it's always been."

"You're full of shit."

Ring Ring...

"Is that your whore calling to tell you goodnight?" Regina says and damn it.. It was Dani calling.. I push the ignore button. "Oh no.. Answer for you whore.. She needs to hear your voice before she lay that head of hers down tonight." She says and now I'm pissed..

"Lose the attitude and stop all this bull shit right now.." I say walking towards her face.. "I mean it." She just smiles at me when I get close to her face. Damn I love this woman.. Why tha fuck would she think I want someone else?

Fuck!! I have a boner.!!

"Maybe you should take a cold shower Miss Swan.. Us talking about your Whore has gotten you excited." She says brushing her ass against me and walking off.. That pisses me off so grab her by her arm and pick her up over my shoulder.. "Put me down Emma!" She yells.

"I will as soon as I get you where I want you."

"Miss Swan." She says once we reach our bedroom..

"And that Miss Swan shit ends tonight Madam Mayor." I throw her on the bed and shut our door.. My good she doesn't have on any panties..

"(Gasps) Mmm.."

Ring Ring...

"Your whore is coming Miss Swan." She says and I throw my phone against the wall and break it.

"STOP CALLING ME THAT!! IT'S SWAN-MILLS!"

"It hasn't been lately."

"What do you want from me?"

"Show me you love me and not her."

"That's easy.. Because I don't love her.. I love you and you know that.. Tell me what you need?" I say climbing on top of her.

"Mi Amor." She whispers and I see her eyes watering..

"Mmm.. Yes baby?" I say kissing her tears away.

"Show me you love me." She's now crying.. And I know exactly what she needs..

CHAPTER 4

"Mi Amor." She whispers and I see her eyes watering..

"Mmm.. Yes baby?" I say kissing her tears away.

"Show me you love me." She's now crying.. And I know exactly what she needs.. I get up and push play on the music..

Whoa, whoa, whoa, yeahWhoa, whoa, whoa, yeah ohWhoa, oh, oh, yeah yeah

She watches me as I take my clothes off.. She's just wearing a robe so she's not wearing much.. I position myself back on top of her and untie her robe..

"I love you Gina." I whisper against her lips before sliding in her.

"(Gasps) Mmm. (Moans)."

Take off those heels, lay on my bedWhisper dirty secrets while I'm pulling on your hairPoison in our veins, but we don't even careCandles dripping on your body, baby this ain't truth or dareEverybody wonders where we run off toMy body on your body, baby sticking like some glueNaughty, let's get naughty, girl it's only one or twoThe fevers fucking running, feel the heat between us two!

"(Moans) I'll never leave you.. Ah!! Fuck!! You're all mine and you're all I need." I whisper in her ear.

"(Moans) Emma."

"Yes baby."

"Mmmm.. (Gasps) Don't stop."

"I'll never stop baby."

I'm gon' ride, I'm gon' rideI'm gon' ride, I'm, I'm gon' ride on you babyOn you lady, all night, all night!I'm gonna take care of your body,I'll be gentle, don't you screamGetting hotter, make it softer,Feel your chest on top of me.I'm gon' ride, I'm gon' rideI'm gon' ride, I'm, I'm gon' ride on you babyOn you lady, all night, all night!I'm gon' make you feel that loving,Getting weak all in your knees.Kiss your body from the tip-top,All the way down to your feet!

"Look at me Gina." I say and she makes eye contact with me.. "(Moans) Just like that baby."

"(Moans) Oh Emma.. Yes.. Right there." Her nails are digging so fucking deep in my back.

"(Groans) Fuck!! Gina." My eyes start to close as I'm about to cum and she flips us so she's on top.. Damn I love this view..

"Ah!! Mmm.. I love you so much" I say and she puts her hand over my mouth and rides me slowly.

"(Moans) Emma.." She moans my name and I love it.

Whoa, and we can go slow,Yeah we can go slow, oh, oh, ohLay on your back, you like it right thereDon't have to say it twiceLove, there's nothing here to fearTaking it back, back to where it's clearRolling on and on, sounds of love are in the air!

I'm gon' ride, I'm gon' rideI'm gon' ride, I'm, I'm gon' ride on you babyOn you lady, all night, all night!I'm gonna take care of your body,I'll be gentle, don't you screamIt's getting hotter, make it softer,Feel your chest on top of me.I'm gon' ride, I'm gon' rideI'm gon' ride, I'm, I'm gon' ride on you babyOn you lady, all night, all night!I'm gon' make you feel that loving,Getting weak all in your knees.Kiss your body from the tip-top,All the way down to your feet!

La, la, whoa, yeah

"AH!!! FUCK BABY!! GINA!"

"(Passionate Screams) Emma.. Ah!! (Moans) I'm gonna cum again."

"Mmm.. Whenever you're ready baby.. (Moans) Whenever you're ready."

"I'm ready now.." She rides me so fast I know I came twice.

Sun's coming up, ohYou're on my side, ohI rub your thighs, ohYou look in my eyes, ohAnd I just see the skies (See the skies)I'm so high but I ain't smoked yet,I'm just coming down from this!

"Fuck!!! Emma please.. (Moans).."

"Yes baby.. I love you "

"Mmmm.. (Moans) Say it again."

"Ahh!!! I love you Gina."

I'm gon' ride, I'm gon' rideI'm gon' ride, I'm, I'm gon' ride on you babyOn you lady, on you lady, all night, all night!I'm gonna take care of your body,I'll be gentle, don't you screamIt's getting hotter, make it softer,Feel your chest on top of me.I'm gon' ride, I'm gon' rideI'm gon' ride, I'm, I'm gon' ride on you babyOn you lady, all night, all night!I'm gon' make you feel that loving,Getting weak all in your knees.Kiss your body from the tip-top,All the way down to your feet!

"(Panting) Mi Amor.. (Moans) Emma." I feel her shaking when I grab her hips.

"Baby.. I got you." I sit up and hold her close as I flip us over so I can pull out.

"(Moans) Emma?" She whispers..

"Yeah baby?" I ask before I turn the music off..

"I'm.. (Crying) Are you going to leave me?"

"Regina stop.. I'm not going anywhere.."

"So there's no one else?"

"No baby?"

"Who were you texting this morning?"

"Killian I swear.. I asked him if he could work night shift and he said no because he was as going to be working on his woman all night."

"Okay.. I only got jealous because you were laughing and you told me it was no one when I asked you who was it."

"Because he is no one.. He just works for me."

"I don't want you running with Danielle in the mornings no more.."

"Baby I swear I'm.."

"Please.. Just don't do it.

"I promise."

"Thank you mi amor."

"Anything for you beautiful."

"I'm sorry I was such a bitch.. It's just the thought of someone else taking you from me is.. I can't take it Emma.. You're mine.. (Crying)."

"Baby stop crying please.. I am yours.. And only yours."

"Okay.. (Sniffs)."

"And you better mines and mine only."

"Yes Mrs. Swan-Mills."

"Thank you baby."

"Let's get dressed and get back down stairs.. I'm pretty sure the kid are back."

"Right.. Let's go baby." I help her out the bed and we go down stairs once we are both dressed.

CHAPTER 5

I wake up to my beautiful wife bending over to pick up her robe.

"Mmm.. Morning beautiful." I say to Regina.

"Morning dear. Breakfast will be ready soon.. You go shower and meet me down there."

"Yes ma'am.." I say smiling.

"Why are you smiling?" She asks me.

"Because I love you and last night was amazing."

"I agree and I love you too baby." She leans down and kiss me.

"You're so sexy." I whisper.

"(Laughs) Thank you.. And you're not so bad yourself."

"Mmmm.. I think I need that cold shower now." I say running to the bathroom.

"(Laughs) You go do that dear."

"Not funny babe." I say before shutting the door.

Later That Day

"Danielle come you come here please?" I yell and get no answer.

"Dani!" I yell.

Knock Knock

"Come in." I say walking around to the closet that's in my office. "Hey Danielle can you do me a favor and.. (Gasps)." I pause at the view I turned around to. "Danielle what the fuck are doing?" I asked..

She's fucking naked!! She's in just her underwear and bra...

"Emma I know you like me."

"Dani I'm married and I love my wife."

"Then why does she has trust issues about you? She already thinks we are fucking each other.. Why not act on it."

"I love my wife and I am not going to cheat on her and I told her last night and she trust me.. Put on some clothes." I say and walks over to me. "Danielle I'm serious."

"I am too." She pushes me down on chair and straddles me.

"Danielle get off me." She then kiss me.. "Fuck!" I yell.

"Emma why do you keep pushing me away?"

"Because I'm married.. I told you.. Hell you know I'm married."

"I know baby but I don't care."

"I really don't want to hurt you."

"Mmmm.. Please do baby."

"Danielle." I trying to get up but she handcuffed me. "Fuck Dani let me up I have a wife."

"And I told you I don't care." She leans in kissing my neck..

"Dani please stop I have a.."

"A wife yeah you keep saying."

"Danielle please stop.. Uncuff me."

"Mmmm.. I heard why a lot of women want to jump your bones."

"I bet you did.. Now get off of me." She reaches for my pants and undo my belt buckle. "Don't do that." I whisper.

"I just want to see for myself.. I know you want me." She reaches in my pants and grab a hold of my shit.. "Mmmmm.. Dani stop."

"Holly shit!! You're big.. Like.. You're not even hard and you are huge.. No wonder your wife has trust issues.. I wouldn't let you out the house.."

"Dani get off of me."

"And if I don't?" She leans in and kiss my neck again.

"Dani I.."

"Emma?" I look up and I see Regina.. Fuck!!! Fuck!!! Fuck!!!

"Baby I swear this is not what it looks like."

"Hello Madam Mayor." Danielle says.

"Get off of me.. And un cuff me now." I say and she gets up and takes them off.

"Regina listen to me."

"There's nothing to say to you Emma.. Goodbye." She then walks off and I run after her trying to fix my pants all at once.

"Regina baby please let me explain." I caught up with her and grabbed her arm.

"Let go of me Mrs. Swan." She says and I hate when she calls me that.

"Don't call me that."

"Mrs. Swan let go of me right now." She says and it's a look in her eyes that I have never seen before.. It's pain and suffering all together.. She's hurt..

"Baby." I whisper before she putted away from me.

"We're done." She says and she gets in her car and drive off..

"REGINA!!" I yell.

"Is she really that mad?" Danielle says behind.

"What the fuck is your problem?"

"It's not a secret that she doesn't make you happy.. I can do more than she has ever done.. I know you want me.. So just take me."

"You sound like a whore.. That's not my type and even if I wasn't married, I wouldn't go for you.. Turn in your badge and gun.. Youre fired." I say walking off.

"Boss you alright? We heard yelling upstairs?" Killian asks.

"I'm fine.. You're in charge until I get back.. Take her badge and gun.. She fired."

"Yes ma'am." Killian says walking towards her and I get in my car and drive home.

At Home

"Regina!" I yell once I get in the house.. She doesn't answer me so for upstairs to our room.. "Regina I'm.."

"Pack your shit and get the fuck out." She says.

"Baby listen to me.. I swear it was not what you think.. I swear."

"Pack your shit.. Or we'll pack ours."

"Who the fuck are we?" I ask.

"Me and my kids."

"Our kids Regina.. Ours."

"Oh so they are your kids?"

"Don't fucking play with me.. Yes they are my kids."

"(Laughs) Oh.."

"What the fuck does that mean?"

"Mom.. What's going on?" Henry ask.

"Nothing.. Go to your room." Regina says.

"Ma?" He then looks at me.

"You heard your mother kid.. Go to your room."

"Why are you guys fighting?"

"Why don't you answer him Emma.. Tell him how I walked in and saw that whore on your lap?"

"Regina stop." I say because I don't want my son hearing this bull shit.

"You cheated on mom? Why?" He asks.

"I didn't cheat on your mother."

"You told me to treat a woman with respect and that's what I always do and here you are sleeping around with some whore?"

"Henry watch your mouth and I wasn't sleeping around.. Regina you have to believe me."

"I don't have to do shit.. Now get the packing or we will."

"You're not taking my kids from me."

"Then get the packing."

"And I'm not leaving?" I say.

"Henry go pack and tell Samantha to do the same."

"What are you two fighting about now.. Because I swear I will bring my grades up.. It's not like I have all Fs." Sam walks in and say.

"Ma is cheating on mom." Henry says.

"I am not cheating on your mother!" I yell.

"Are you serious?" Sam asks me.

"I didn't cheat on your mother.. She just saw something she shouldn't have."

"Oh I get it.. So if I didn't see what was going on then it wouldn't have been a problem?"

"That's not what I am saying.. I.."

"What er you talking about.. Who did you cheat on mom with."

"It was nobody.. I didn't cheat on her.. She walked in and Dani was on my lap and.."

"You're sleeping with Danielle?" Sam asks.

"Oh so our children knows who this whore is? Samantha how do you know Danielle?"

"She came here with ma before."

"So you brought the whore into our home?" Regina asks.

"Regina it's not like that.. I was.."

"Samantha go pack and meet me down stairs.. Henry you too." Regina says cutting me off.

"You're not taking my kids away from me." I say to Regina.

"THEN PACK YOUR SHIT EMMA!!" She yells.

"Youre not even going to let me explain?" I ask.

"Like I told you at your office. There is nothing to talk about.. Here." She says and she hands me divorce papers.

"Regina come on.. You can't be serious."

"Go to the last page and ask me again if I'm serious."

"You signed these?"

"I sure did and Susan, our family lawyer will be here in the morning.. So it would be nice if you would go ahead and sign them right now please."

"Fuck you for signing these and I'm not signing shit." I say and I rip them up in her face.

"That's fine dear.. So are you doing to pack or us because one of us is leaving.. You or me and my kids."

"Ma?" She says and I look at when and she is crying.

"Baby don't cry this is all just a miss understanding.. I swear to you I didn't cheat on your mother." I say to her.

"So we're moving?" Henry asks and I look at Regina.

"No.. I'm leaving." I say walking to the closet and pack me a few bags.

"Thank you." Regina says walking out today the room wotht the kids... Once I'm down packing I walk down stairs and they were sitting on the couch.

"Regina I promise I didn't cheat on you.. And I am truly sorry for what you saw.. I really am.. I love you Regina." I say walking out of the door.

"Ma!" Sam yells and I turn around and she hugs me tight. "Please don't go."

"I have to baby.. I love you and tell your brother I love him too." I say.

"Okay." She let's me go and she runs in the house and shuts the door.

CHAPTER 6

It's been almost 2 months and Regina still doesn't believe me and she has a new love interest in her life. Like how the fuck can you move on so fast after all the years we were together???? But fuck it, I've been trying and trying and my own children told me I didn't try hard enough.. That shit really hurt. But what can I do? I've apologize over and over again.. I call her phone and she doesn't answer and when it's time to do inspection and gather all the paperwork, she sends someone else to do it.. Like what the fuck man.. But I'm done stressing out about this shit and I'm signing those fucking papers.

"Hey boss you want to grab a drink with the team?" Killian asks.

"Hell sure why not." I say.

"You can ride with me because I'm not drinking tonight, I have to be back in 8 hours."

"That's Jones I'll meet you outside."

"Sure thing boss." He says before he closes my office door and gather my things.

Hours Later

"I mean you come here every Friday night.. You must be looking for something." The young woman says to me.

"Just a drink that's all."

"Nothing else?"

"No ma'am.. Can I have my tab please?"

"Oh no baby.. It's on me tonight."

"No thank you.. He's $100 bucks.. Have a good night and keep the change."

"See you next Friday."

"Maybe." I yell back over the music." I drive myself home because I decided not to ride with Killian.. He has to be at work early so I wasn't going to keep him out a night because of me and I leave pretty close so I'll can handle the driving.

"Ma?" I look up and I see Sam at my front door.

"Baby what are you doing here? It's after midnight?

"I couldn't sleep."

"Why not?"

"I prefer not to say."

"You can tell me I won't bite your head off like your mother would."

"No seriously I'm going to say, can I sleep in my room tonight I left my house key to your house on my bed."

"Only if you tell me what's been keeping you up at night.. Baby it's not good stressing out.. Is it because of school? I mean I can get a someone to help you study and.."

"Ma no it's not school okay?"

"Then what is it?" I ask and she looks at the ground. "Samantha?"

"Mom and her boyfriend were you know and.. Whatever never-mind.. I'm tired can I please go lay down."

"Your mother and her boyfriend were what??" I ask and she gives me the 'Ma really?' look.. "Oh.. Okay.. So you mean they were.. Okay."

"Sorry that's why I'd dint want to tell you but I can't sleep so I can please go to my room?"

"Of course baby.. Get you some rest."

"Thanks ma.. I love you."

"I love you too."

The Next Day

"Boss I thought you were off today?"

"Yeah I am.. I just wanted to get the paperwork done for the Mayor."
I say and everyone just looks at me with a sad face.

"Right.. We'll were about to go check out the Rabbit Hole.. They
reported a fight." Killian says.

"Okay and be careful.. Killian take off when you get back."

"You got it boss." They leave and moments later Regina and her
boyfriend walks in..

"(Laughing) You have a very dirty."

"(Clears Throat) Regina darling.. We have a guest." The boyfriend
says.

"Em.. Emma?"

"Here's your paperwork Madam Mayor." I say handing it to her
without eye contact.

"Ugh.. Thank You."

"No problem." I then walk to my office."

"Emma can I speak to you in private."

"No Regina.. But it is about my children then yes, but if not, then we have nothing to discuss Madam Mayor." I say looking at her and she's fucking beautiful.. And something about her has changed.. I know that look.. FUCK!!! "Congratulations." I say to her.

"Excuse me?" She asks.

"On the pregnancy.. Congratulations." I say and her eyes widen and her boyfriend looks at her.

"I'm not.. I'm not pregnant"

"Regina why didn't you tell me?" He asks.

"Robin I'm no pregnant."

"Yes you are and I'm sorry.. I honestly thought you knew.. I'm sorry."

"Emma I'm not pregnant.. Robin we should go."

"I know that glow you get when you're pregnant Gina.. And you Madam Mayor are pregnant.. Congratulations to the both of you." I say before I shut my office door.. Fuck!! I'm suppose to give he babies not this Robin man.. "(Crying) Fuck!" I knock all of the papers off my desk..

Knock Knock

"(Clears Throat) Yeah."

"Emma it's me can I come in?"

"No Regina.. Go with your boyfriend." I say and she walks in.

"Emma." She walks in and see me crying. "Emma can we talk about this? I told Robin I would meet him at home."

"Home.. So he moved on already.. You sure moved on fast."

"Emma I'm sorry that you're hurting.. I truly am, but you hurt me first."

"I didn't do shit!! And tried to explain myself but you didn't want to listen."

"I saw you."

"I don't give a damn what you saw, you shout have trusted me because I would have let you explain."

"Emma I'm sorry."

"No you're not, now go home to your boyfriend, I'm sure he'll be waiting to celebrate your pregnancy."

"I'm not pregnant."

"Regina I know when you're pregnant.. I know that beautiful glow you get when you pregnant.. Go take a test and I I'm wrong then

I'm sorry.. It just hurt to see you with someone else and to know that you're carrying his baby makes my heart stop.. I feeling like I'm fucking dying Regina. (Crying) Now get out of my office please."

"I'm sorry." She says and she walks away.

"Yeah me too." I say before she shuts the door.

Regina POV

"Hello Madam Mayor." The doctor says.

"Hello dear how are you?"

"I'm fine thank you. What can I do for you today?"

"I need to speak with Rebecca."

"Okay you can go ahead and go to her office.. I'll let her know that you are here."

"Thank you."

"Yes ma'am." I walk to her office and her door is already open.

"Regina how lovely it is to see you."

"Rebecca hello.. I'm sorry to just show up unexpectedly but do you mind running a few test on me.. I might be pregnant."

"Sure have a seat and I'll do a little blood work." She walk over to her cabinet and gets everything she need s and she takes my blood. "Okay I'll get these down to the lab and I'll be right back."

"Okay dear.. Thank you."

"No problem."

20 Minutes Later

"Okay Regina you are pregnant and it looks like you are about 14 and a half weeks." Shit!!! This is Emma's baby.

"Oh.. Okay." I say a little shocked.

"I'm sorry you don't seem happy."

"Oh no.. I mean yes.. Yes I'm happy it's just a little surprising that's all."

"I understand.. Here is your paperwork.. I'll see you in a few weeks for your check up."

"Thank you Rebecca."

"You're welcome.. Have a good afternoon Regina."

"Thank you and you do the same dear." I say and walk out the building and go to my car. "What the fuck!" I yell when my door is closed.

Chapter 7

R egina POV

"Mom!" Henry tells.

"Yes dear?"

"Have you see my cel phone?"

"It's on the couch. Hurry up we have to go."

"Good morning love. How was the appointment yesterday?"

"Ugh good."

"So are you pregnant?" He ask with a smile on his face.

"Yeah."

"How far along are you?"

"Ugh.. I forgot.. Like 8 I think.. So that would make me two months."
I lie because if I say I'm 14 weeks then he would know this is Emma's
baby.

"I'm so happy baby." He leans in to kiss me.

"What are we happy about?" Sam asks.

"Nothing I'm.."

"Your mom and I are having a baby." Robin says.. Shit!!!!!

"Are you fucking serious?" Sam asks me.

"Excuse me? You better watch your tone on how you talk to me and
stop cursing."

"Whatever." She says and walks away.

"Samantha get back here." I say and she keeps walking.

"Sam your mother was talking to you." I look up and see Emma
standing there.

"She's pregnant with his baby." Sam says.

"I know.. Now apologize to your mother.. Apologize to the both of
them."

"But.."

"No buts.. Now." Emma says.

"Sorry Ma.. Sorry Robin.. Congratulations I guess."

"What's happening?" Henry asks.

"Robin got ma pregnant and she's keeping it."

"You're joking? You're having a baby with him? Mom do something." He says.

"I can't.. She's with him now.. Go get your bags.. You too Sam." Emma tells them and they leave and go upstairs.

"Robin can I have a minute alone with Emma please?"

"Yes.. I'm headed out for work so I'll see you later." He kisses me goodbye and the look on Emma's face was nothing but hurt.. She's not anger or anything.. All I see is hurt in her eyes..

"Bye Emma." Robin says.

"Bye." She whispers.

"Emma?" I say and she doesn't look at me.

"Emma can you please just.."

"Please what Regina?" Emma says.

"I'm sorry. I didn't know he was going to do that in front of you."

"Of course you didn't.. Did you know he was putting a baby inside of you when you were fucking him?"

"Emma don't do this.. Not while.."

"Not while what?? While the kids are here? I mean you do fuck him when they're here trying to sleep at night."

"Excuse me?" I say.

"Yeah.. Sam showed up at my place because she couldn't sleep.. Apparently you and Robin were having fun as he call it."

"Emma I'm sorry."

"Don't apologize to me.. Say sorry to our children."

"I'm sorry I hurt you." I say.

"Why? I mean I did hurt you first right? At least that's what you think."

"Emma I saw.."

"You saw what!? A thirsty bitch force her hand in my pants? But hey, let you tell it I was fucking her the whole time."

"Emma please just.."

"What? I mean did you even look at the cameras from that day?" She asks.

"What?" I question.

"The cameras you put in my office.. Did you watch it to see what really happened?"

"I ugh.. No." I whisper.

"Of course you didn't.. Kids let's go." She yells upstairs. "Maybe you should go have a look at it.. Make sure the volume is turned up to the max." And with that she was out the front door and the kids was not to far behind her.

•••

"I love my wife." Emma says.

"Then why does she has trust issues about you? She already thinks we are fucking each other.. Why not act on it."

"I love my wife and I am not going to cheat on her and I told her last night and she trust me.. Put on some clothes." Emma says and Danielle walks over to her. "Danielle I'm serious."

"I am too." She pushes her down on chair and straddles her.

"Danielle get off me." She then kiss her.. "Fuck!" She yell.

"Emma why do you keep pushing me away?"

"Because I'm married.. I told you.. Hell you know I'm married."

"I know baby but I don't care."

"I really don't want to hurt you."

"Mmmm.. Please do baby."

"Danielle." She's trying to get up but she handcuffed her. "Fuck Dani let me up I have a wife."

"And I told you I don't care." She leans in kissing her neck..

"Dani please stop I have a.."

"A wife yeah you keep saying."

"Danielle please stop.. Uncuff me."

"Mmmm.. I heard why a lot of women want to jump your bones."

"I bet you did.. Now get off of me." She reaches for her pants and undo her belt buckle. "Don't do that." Emma whisper.

"I just want to see for myself.. I know you want me." She reaches in her pants and grab a hold of her shit..

"Mmmmm.. Dani stop."

"Holly shit!! You're big.. Like.. You're not even hard and you are huge.. No wonder your wife has trust issues.. I wouldn't let you out the house.."

"Dani get off of me."

"And if I don't?" She leans in and kiss her neck again.

"Dani I.."

●●

I ended the video right there..

"Fuck she was telling the truth."

"Who was?" Robin asks from the door way.

"(Clears Throat) Ugh no one.. What are you doing here at my office? I thought you had work?"

"I do.. I just wanted to check on you."

"Oh.. Well I'm fine.." I say going to back to signing some paper work.

"I brought lunch." He says with a smile.

"Thanks honey." I whisper.

"You're welcome." He says and he sits down in front of me and we ate lunch and talked about how I feel l.

Fuck this is Emma's baby and she told me the truth.. She'll never forgive me for this..

FUCK

CHAPTER 8

E mma POV

"Emma."

"Regina what are you doing here?" I ask when I come from my office.

"Can we talk?"

"Is the kids okay?"

"What? Yes of course.. They're fine."

"Then what is it because I'm in the middle of something and.."

"Hey babe I left my drink in the car.. Could you.. Oh sorry."

"Gabrielle? Wait are you two.."

"Ugh Madam Mayor I'm.." Gabby starts but I interrupt.

"No Gabby it's okay.. Regina I told her not to tell you."

"What that you're fucking my assistant?" She snaps.

"Hold on a second because I haven't fucked no body.. You the one jumped in a relationship and went right to fucking.. And now you're knocked up.. I'm not that easy.. And who I'm in a relationship with is none of your business.. I don't care that she works for you."

"You're right." She whispers.. "But I'm not easy."

"What do you want Regina?"

"To talk to you."

"Okay talk."

"Hey Em.. I'm going to the car and get my drink.. I'll be back in a few minutes.. I'll give you two some privacy." Gabby says.

"You don't have to do that." I say.

"No it's fine."

"Okay babe.. I won't be long."

"Okay." She smiles at Regina and walks out the door.

"What is it?"

"I watched it."

"You watched what?"

"I watched the video recording of that day from your office."

"(Laughs) And what did you see? What did you hear?" I ask and she has tears coming down her face.

"I saw her trying to seduce you and I heard you tell her no and that you were married and you love me."

"You sure that's what you saw and heard because last I checked I cheated on you that day and I was fucking her the entire time."

"Emma I'm sorry."

"Yeah.. Me too.. I'm happy you watched it because ow you know that you made a huge mistake.. Now if you don't mind I was having lunch with my girlfriend." I say and her eyes darkened.

"Emma I'm sorry."

"Yeah I heard you Regina."

"So you and Gabby huh?"

"Yes me and Gabby.. Are you going to extend my lunch hour or are we done?" I hate to be mean but I'm pissed off.

"I was hoping that we could maybe talk and.."

"Regina I'm not running back to you after you let that boy of a man knock you up and now he's living in a house that I paid for.. Save it..

Go back to your new man and leave me the hell alone." I mange to say before tears start to run down my face. "(Crying) You broke me Regina.. You fucking broke me.. Every since I laid eyes on you, all I've ever wanted was you.. And for you to think I'm a liar is fucking heart breaking.. You should have known I wasn't lying.. Hell I even told you I was being faithful and then I made love to you that night.. It was amazing, and for you think I want someone else is insane.. And what really hurts the worst is to see you carrying his fucking baby.. Now that is even more hurtful.. Good bye Madam Mayor.. I do believe I was having lunch." I say and Gabby walks back in.

"Are you okay Em?" She asks.

"I'm fine babe.. Let's get back to lunch, Regina was just leaving." I say.

"Yes.. (Clear Throat) See you in the morning Miss Banks." Regina says and she walks away.

"Are you sure you're okay?" She asks again.

"If you kiss me I'll be even better." She laughs and kiss me. "I'm much better now."

"Good.. Lets eat before you have to go back out on the street."

"Deal."

•••••••••••• Later That Night ••••••••••••

"We don't have to do this Emma." Gabby says.

"It's fine.. Unless you don't want to.. I'm sorry are we moving to fast?" I ask.

"No baby.. He'll no.. I can't wait to be with."

"Me too, it just I haven't.."

"I know.. Been with no one since Regina?" She asks.

"Yes."

"Okay that's fine.. We take it as slow as you want to baby." She gets off the counter top and manage to rub her ass against me ass she's walking away.

"Mmm.. You're teasing me." I whisper.

"Just letting you know two can play that." She smiles back.

"Excuse me?" I ask smiling.

"You walk around in those sweat pants all day and expect me not to see your big ass print from your dick."

"(Laughing) Baby I can't help it if I'm big.. I can't control it."

"Looks at you Emma.. You fucking hard right now and we.. Fuck!"

"If you're not ready for it I understand."

"It's not that.. It's just.."

"Too big for you?" I ask with a smile.

"Oh I can take it." She says

"Oh I know you can baby."

"How about you take me upstairs and have your way with me."

"Yes ma'am" I waste no time to pick her up and carrying her to my bedroom..

CHAPTER 9

"E mma have you seen my shirt?" Gabby ask.

"No but it looks better off your body."

"(Laughs) Funny, but I have to have my shirt.. I can't walk out of here without it."

"You don't have to leave at all."

"I have work."

"Regina will understand that you can't make it today.. Just call her and say you spent the night at my place.. She'll get the hint."

"How do you know?"

"Because she's been in the same position.. I'm a beast in bed and I know you're sore." I smile at her.

"Yes I'm sore and I need to go to work Miss Swan."

"Mmm.. I like it when you call me that."

"Is that so daddy."

"Woah.. Slow down with the dirty nicknames.. Now I have a boner."

"I can help you with that?" She says.

"No.. You don't have to do that."

"What if I wanted too."

"Gabby you are not giving me head."

"You ate me out 4 times and I can't suck your dick? Please daddy." She begs against my lips. "Please."

"I can take care of it." I whisper.

"Fine but do you remember how good you said I taste?"

"Yeah."

"Good.. Because you're not going down on me again."

"(Laughs) You're joking." I state.

"We'll see.. And I found my shirt." She leans in and kiss me.

"Oh yeah?? Where is it??"

"Underneath your pretty little ass." She says.

"You got me." I smile and give it to her.

"Thank you."

"You're welcome.. And I'm keeping these." I say holding up her panties.

"I nee those."

"I'm sure you have more at your place."

"Bye Emma."

"Bye babe."

————————Regina's Office ———————

"Emma what are you doing here?" Regina says.

"I'm here to see Gabby." I say.

"She's on a business call right now.. Do you want to leave a message?" She says with an attitude.. And I know just what to do with that attitude because two can play a childish ass game.

"Sure.. Tell her she left her panties in my bed." I say putting them in Regina's suit jacket that she is wearing.

"So you are sleeping with her?"

"Of course I am.. She is my girlfriend.. Aren't you fucking your little boy toy?"

"Emma I really need to speak with you about something important."

"Are the kids okay?"

"What?? Yeah."

"Is it about the station?"

"No Emma it's.."

"Then we have nothing to take about.. Tell Gabby my place at 5pm and please don't e late."

"Gabby is staying over today.. I have somewhere to be."

"Then cancel.. I need Gabby at 5pm."

"Emma she's working late today.. End of discussion."

"I will come down there and get her. Remember when you were late and I came and got you?? Now what makes you think I won't come for her?"

"Fine.. I'll get someone to cover for her."

"Now was that so hard Regina?"

"Emma I.."

"Bye Regina and don't forget to tell her she left her panties in my bed."

——————————5pm——————————

"EMMA!" I hear Gabby yells my name from the front door.

"I'm in the kitchen babe."

"What the hell is wrong with you?"

"Nothing I'm fine."

"You're fine?? Well that's great because I'm not fine."

"What's wrong?" I already knowing what she is mad about.

"What's wrong is my boss just handed me my panties in front of the entire staff."

"Okay."

"Okay??? Emma that was embarrassing."

"No what's embarrassing is Regina and the only reason I did that was to piss her off.. She was acting like a bitch and I gave her your panties and told her to tell you that you.."

"Yeah that I left them in your bed.. Yeah I know."

"I don't see the problem.. She is the one who is embarrassed and mad that her assistant got my attention and I'm no longer focusing on her."

"No Emma.. That's not the point.. My point is everyone is looking at me like I fucked you on the first night."

"But we didn't ."

"They don't know that."

"Fuck what people think.. We know the truth."

"Emma please don't do that again.. Please."

"I'm sorry.. How can I make it up to you?" I ask once I turn the oven off.

"I can think of something." She smiles.

"Gabby no.. You don't have to do that to please me."

"What if I need to do it."

"Why do you need to do it."

"I want to know what it feels like to have power over you."

"Wow.. And you want to do that with my dick in your mouth?"

"Yes."

"Oh.. Well that's a first."

"I can take it daddy."

"What the fuck?? Gabby baby please stop with the nicknames."

"Why papi.. Don't you like it." She called me Papi and the only person who's ever called me that was Gina. "You okay baby?"

"I'm fine.. Are you hungry?"

"Not for food.. I want you."

"You got me." I say.

"I want you in my mouth."

"(Laughs) Gabby baby.. You don't.."

"I heard you the first time and other times after that.. I don't have to do that, but I want too."

"We haven't been together long enough for you to do that.."

"But you can do it for me?"

"It's different.. For women it's special when they feel their orgasm takes over.. For men it's just.. I don't know.. Well once I get a boner I immediately want the ache to go away, but with women I like to take my time and show them how special they are.. I don't care how I get rid of mine.. I just want you to feel good."

"You do make me feel good.. I just wish I could repay the favor."

"You did repay the favor.. You took it like I knew you would.. And I know I'm big and I know it's not easy to get used to my size but you took it good and I like how you took control and got on top of me and started riding me.. Now that was sexy."

"I'm so wet right now."

"I could take care of that for you."

"No thank you.. I can do it later.. Let's eat." She walks pass me and goes to fix her plate and I just stare at her. "You coming?" She ask.

"(Clears Throat) Ye.. Yeah.. Coming." What have I gotten myself into?????

CHAPTER 10

———— Two Months Later ————————

Regina's POV

"Are you okay Gabby?" I ask.

"Yes ma'am.. I'm fine.."

"You just throw up." I say.

"Yes.. Maybe it's something I ate."

"Of course."

"Can I go on break early?? I need to go home and change."

"Sure."

"Thank you." She says and walks out.. I'm calling Emma because I know she's not pregnant.

"Hello Madam Mayor.. What can I do for you?" Emma says.

"Your girlfriend had to leave for break 4 hours early today."

"What?? Is she okay?"

"I don't know Emma.. You tell me.. She's is throwing up.. She did today yesterday and the other day."

"Okay.. Maybe she caught the bug or something."

"Yeah.. She caught something and I don't think it was the bug."

"Well what is it Regina?"

"Pregnant maybe."

"Fuck you Regina for even saying that because I.. We.. Fuck!" Emma yells.

"What's wrong Emma?" I laugh. "Forgot to wrap it up?"

"Her pussy is to good for me to wrap it up.. I like to fuck her raw because I love the way she feels.. Goodbye Madam Mayor."

"Fuck you Emma." I say before hanging up the phone..

Emma's POV

"Gabby?!" I yell once I get in the house.

"Emma what are you doing home so early?"

"Are you pregnant?" I ask and she sits down at the table and start playing with her fingers. "Gabby?"

"What?" She says.

"Are you pregnant?"

"Emma I don't want to talk about this right now."

"Are you pregnant?? Yes or no?"

"Yes."

"Shit." I say.

"Yeah.. I know you don't want another kid and not with me anyway."

"Hey I never said that."

"You didn't have too."

"Gabby I'm.."

"I know you still love her.. I can see it on your face when you look at her and when the two of you argue, I can see it."

"Gabby there will alway be apart of me that loves Regina.. She is the mother of my kids.. I was married to her for over eighteen years.. We've been together for more.. And I love you."

"You what?"

" I said I.."

"No I heard you.. Are you saying this because I'm pregnant?"

"No."

"Yes you are."

"No I'm not.. I love you Gabrielle."

"I love you too Emma."

"So were on the same page.. How far along are you?"

"Six weeks."

"Wow.. Why didn't you tell me?"

"Because I wasn't sure if you wanted another kid. Especially with me?"

"Why wouldn't I want a baby with you?"

"Because you're still in love Regina."

"Gabby I.."

"It's okay.. I saw this day coming."

"Oh yeah? Well do you want to know what I saw coming? Or what I didn't see coming?"

"What's that?"

"That I would be lucky enough to find somebody like you. Yes I love Regina. Apart of me will alway love her. She's the mother of my kids. But that doesn't mean I don't love you Gabrielle, because I do. And I'm going to be here for you and the baby. Whatever you need. I got it."

"I'm waiting on my insurance card to come in the mail so I can afford to go to all the appointments. Don't get me wrong, Regina pays me good but I have other bills I have to take care of and let's not for get my rent and my house bills."

"I'll take care of the doctors appointments. I'll pay. How much do you need?"

"I have to have a test run on me to make sure everything is okay because of the car wreck I had five years ago and that test is $5,000 because of the equipment they will use and the operation. So when my insurance card comes in I'll go to the doctor."

"I'll pay for that test run. You wanna go today?"

"Emma no. That's $5,000."

"I know that. I heard you the first time."

"No way. That's too much money."

"Taking care of the woman I love and my baby is more important than a couple of thousand dollars."

"That's a lot of money. Are you sure because I don't know when I'll be able to pay you back."

"Don't be ridiculous Gabby. You don't have to pay me back."

"I have to pay you back. That's a lot of money."

"Just take care of your body and don't forget to give me a kiss before you go to work. That's good enough for me."

"You're crazy."

"Crazy about you baby.. Crazy about you."

"(Laughs) She was stupid."

"Who?" I ask.

"Regina. Because there is no way in hell I would have let you go."

"Well that's her lose and your win."

"You always have the right thing to say."

"Let's go to the hospital. I'll call and tell Regina you're not coming back in today."

"Emma it's Friday. I can't leave her in there by herself."

"I'll send someone over there."

"Okay. Thank you."

"No problem." After call Regina and going to the hospital, me and Gabby decided to order in instead of going out.

"You ready for bed baby?" I ask her.

"Yesssss.. I am sooooo tired."

"Here let me help you." I say walking over to her.

"Babe I'm fine.. I can walk upstairs."

"You sure?"

"Yes. Come with me if you like. You can walk behind just in case I fall."

"I'll never let you hit the ground."

"I know." She turns around to kiss me.

"I love you."

"I love you too Emma." She says getting in the bed. "Goodnight."

"Goodnight Gabby." I reach over and turn the lamp off.

CHaPTer 11

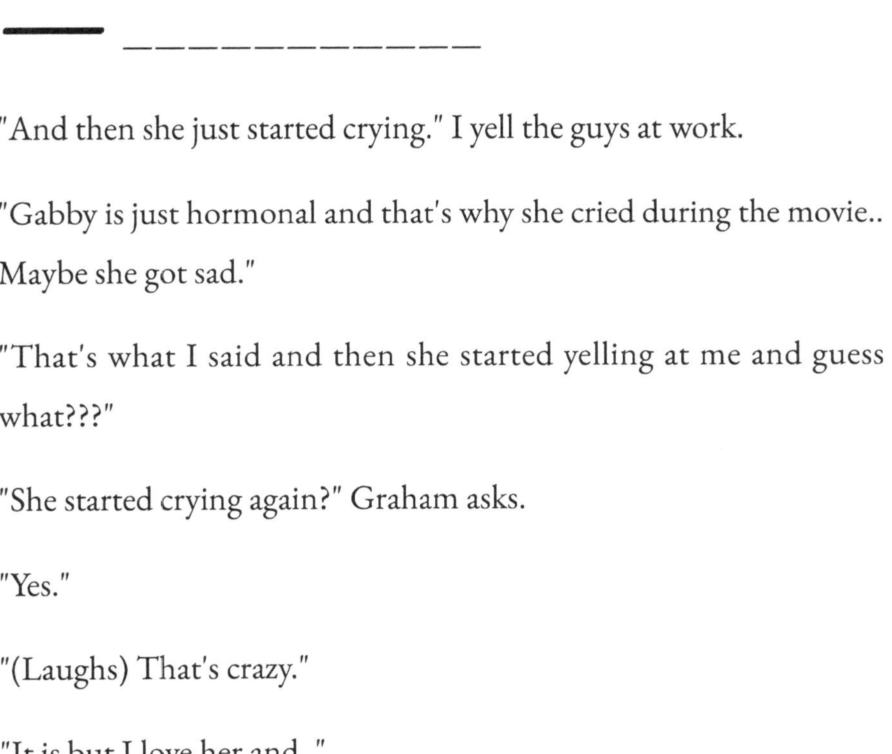

_____________________________—   5   Months   Later
_____   _________________—

"And then she just started crying." I yell the guys at work.

"Gabby is just hormonal and that's why she cried during the movie.. Maybe she got sad."

"That's what I said and then she started yelling at me and guess what???"

"She started crying again?" Graham asks.

"Yes."

"(Laughs) That's crazy."

"It is but I love her and.."

"Madam Mayor Good Morning." Officer Hicks says.

"Morning... Emma can I speak with you?"

"Is it about work or the kids?"

"I need to speak to you in private please."

"Regina I don't have time for this and.."

"Privately Miss Swan." She says and this time I know she is serious.

"We can step out if you want us too boss." Graham says.

"No it's fine.. Regina let's go to my office." I say and once we get in there I ask if she okay..

"I'm fine but Gabby was in a car accident."

"WHAT!?" I yell.

"Emma please calm down."

"Calm down??? Are you serious??? What happened is she okay?? Is the baby okay??"

"Emma I'm so sorry.."

"(Crying) Sorry for what Regina??? Are they okay?" I ask full of emotions.

"Gabby is fine."

"And the baby?"

"Emma please calm down and.."

"For fuck sakes is my baby okay Regina??"

"I'm sorry.. She lost the baby." She says and it's like my whole world fell apart.. "But listen to me Emma.. She needs you right now so you need to pull yourself together and be there for her.. I know this is hard but please.. She is a little stressed and they said they do not need her blood pressure spiking."

"I can't do this again." I whisper.

"Emma I know.. What happed to our baby is.. I know it was a terrible time for us but we had each other and now she needs you.. So let me take you too her and please calm down."

"Okay.. I'm sorry I snapped at you and I'm so sorry Gina."

"It's okay.. I understand what you're feeling and I'm sorry it has happened to you again.. I'm truly sorry Emma."

"Thank you.. And thank you for coming down and tell me."

"You're welcome."

———————————————————————————————————

——————————

"Gabby?" I whisper because she's asleep.

"Emma?" She says back.

"Hey baby." I say.

"I'm so sorry." She says.. "I... (Sniffs) I lost it.. I'm so sorry."

"You have nothing to be sorry for."

"They said I lost her."

"Baby it's okay and.. Wait her??? It was a.. Ugh.. (Clears Throat) It was a girl?" I ask.

"Yes.." She says and I have to turn around because now I'm about to cry. "Emma look at me." She says and I don't turn around. "Do you hate me?" She says that's when I had to turn around.

"What?! I could never hate you.. it's just me and Regina ugh.."

"Are you cheating on me with her?" She asks.

"No Gabby.. We lost our first baby."

"What?"

"Yeah.. It was a boy and the second time we found out she was pregnant the doctor told us they were twins.."

"I'm so sorry.. I never wanted to make you feel this type of pain and to know that it has happened again breaks my heart."

"Please stop saying you are sorry.. Are you okay?"

"I'm fine."

"Gabby it's not healthy to keep stuff like this in.. Let it out and talk to me."

"I'm fine." She rolls over in the bed and looks out the window.

"Gabby please listen to me.. I love you and if.."

"I'm leaving." She said.

"What?? Leaving where?"

"I'm going back home.. My brother is on a plane now to come get me."

"And you wasn't going to talk to me first?"

"I'm talking now."

"I mean before you decided to call and buy a plane ticket??? What about us?"

"I'm sorry but I can't stay here and then look at you everyday and see her face."

"You saw her?"

"She looks like you." She whispers.

"Oh yeah??"

"Yeah.. More like you then Sam."

"(Laughs) I'm sure she's just as beautiful as her mother."

"She still loves you.. Maybe you can work it out now that she knows the truth.."

"But I want you."

"And I also know you want her, but you don't want to break my heart and go be with her.. You'll break my heart if you don't be with her."

"I'm not worried about none of that.. I want to know how you feel and is there something I can do for you Gabby??? Do you need anything??"

"(Crying) Hold me. Please?"

"Of course." I say and I lay beside her on the bed and hold her close. Moments later Regina knocks on the door..

"Come in."

"Sorry to interrupt.. But we got the guy who hit you." She yells Gabby.

"Where is he?" I asks.

"I let the FBI take him in because I knew you was going to act out of impulse."

"See.. I told you she loves you." Gabby whispers in my ear.

"Not now Gabby."

"Everything okay?" Regina asks.

"Yes.. What happened?" I ask.

"He was drinking and texting at the same time and his blood alcohol level was high."

"I'm going to fucking kill him." I say and get up out of the bed.

"Emma wait.." Gabby says.

"Gabby get some rest.. I'll be back." I say and when I opened the door Graham and officer Hicks was there. "Excuse me guys."

"I'm sorry but we can't let you leave."

"I'm your boss I gave you an order." I say.

"And I'm your boss and I gave an order." Regina says.. "Hand Graham your Gun and your badge."

"What?"

"Now Emma.. Please."

"Are you serious?"

"Yes because I'll be damned if my children has to visit you in jail behind bars because you can't control your temper.."

"Fine.. Here and you know he's a dead man Regina??"

"Emma.."

"You know how I used to be when we were younger.. I'm going to fucking kill him.. And I don't give a fuck if the president is his bodyguard.. He can't hide from me.." I hand Graham my badge and gun and them I go back and sit with Gabby.

"Thank you Emma." Regina says.

"Thank you because you know what I'm capable of.. Now do you really think I'm going to let him get away with killing my kid and hurting the woman I love?"

"No.. But I don't want you to give me any details so Goodnight Emma and Good Night Gabby.. I'm truly sorry for you both.." Regina says.

"Thank you." Gabby says.

"Get you some rest and you too Emma.. That's an order for you both.."

"Yes ma'am." Gabby says with a smile.

"Good night Regina." I say before she closes the door. "Get some rest Gabby."

"Will you be here when I wake up?"

"Of course."

"You promise?"

"I promise." I whisper in her ear... Once she is asleep I cry in silence..

CHAPTER 12

"Good Morning." I hear Gabby say.

"Morning.. Ugh should you be up walking around like that?"

"I'm fine Emma.. My brother is here he went to get coffee."

"Why didn't you wake me up?"

"Regina said that you should sleep and to call her when you wake up."

"You don't have to call her."

"To late.. I just texted and informed her that you was awake."

"Thanks babe."

"You're welcome.. Did you want a.."

"Sorry Gabby they didn't have and donuts.. We can get some before he head out.. Hello you must be Emma?"

"That's me.. It's nice to meet you."

"Nice to might you too."

"I'll take you bags to the car and all you stuff is being shipped to mom and dads house."

"Thank you." Gabby tells her brother.

"I'll be outside.. Bye Emma." He says before he takes the bags and go.

"Bye."

"I had the movers to pack my stuff at your place."

"Okay.. I could have helped you know?"

"I know but Regina said not to wake you."

"You don't have to do everything she tells you.. You do know that right?"

"Well as long as she is living in this town she does, but until then.. I hope you have a safe trip back home."

"Thank you."

"You're welcome."

"Gabby I can drive you to the airport." I say.

"No that's okay.. My brother already paid for a driver and you need to do what we talked about.. She's standing right there."

"Gabby!"

"Am I missing something?" Regina asks.

"Emma loves you.. She forgives you but you really hurt her when you thought she would cheat on you.. She wants you back but you're with that guy and she doesn't want to come between you guys.."

"Gabby!! Why would you tell her that?"

"Because you're too stubborn to do it.. So you're welcome and bye Emma.." She says and she walks over to where I was sitting. "One last kiss." She leans in and kiss me.. "I love you.. And I want you happy.. Now get your wife back.. And when I call you, I want to see you with her.. As a matter of fact, I'll FaceTime you." She turns around to Regina. "Bye Miss Mills.. I'm sorry.. Bye Regina."

"Have a safe flight Gabby." Regina says and Gabby leaves and closes the door behind her.

"I should get to work." I say.

"Emma?" Regina whisper.

"I need to go.. You know, so I won't be late."

"I'm your boss and I said you can be late."

"Regina please I.."

"I miss you."

"Don't do that.. You have a new man in your life.. He loves you and.."

"But I love you." She whispers.

"Fuck Regina. Don't do this."

"I'll leave him today if you asked me to."

"No.. And I'll never ask you to do that."

"Even if you get to be happy in the end?"

"Yes.. Because I know what it feels like to lose you and I'll be damned if I am the cause of someone else's pain."

"Emma please.. Let's talk about this."

"I really have to go to work Gina."

"I miss you calling me Gina."

"Regina please let me go."

"You're wrong you know?"

"About what?"

"You think he loves me?? If he loves me then he wouldn't be.. You know what? Never mind."

"He what?"

"Nothing Emma.. It's nothing.. Forget I said anything."

"Did he do something to you?? Did he do something to the kids?? Answer me Regina."

"He just has a temper that's all.. But forget I said anything.. Who knows what he would do if he found out I said something to you.. Or anybody." She walks out the door and follow her out.

"Wait a second what do you mean he.."

"Regina!! There you go. I was looking for you." Speak of the devil.. There he is.

"Sorry Baby.. I was here to check on Emma."

"Is that so?"

"It's not like that I was just.."

"We'll talk about it at home." He walks up and grabs her arm.

"(Laughs) Wow." I say.

"Something funny?" He asks me.

"Are you stupid or just yeah.. Stupid?"

"Excuse me?"

"First you are rude as hell and then you have the audacity to grab my pregnant wife by her arm. Do you have a death wish?"

"Watch your mouth bitch."

"Trust me.. I'm the baddest Bitch you'll ever meet."

"Regina we're leaving now." He pulls her arm harder.

"Ouch.. Ah!! That hurt." Now I'm pissed.

"Stop making a fucking scene." He says to her in her ear.

"You do know I'm carry a gun correct?"

"Does that suppose to scare me?" He says.

"Let her go or I'll light you up like a Christmas tree."

"She's mine." He says.

"What makes you think she's yours?"

"Well she divorced you and she's having my kid."

"Who said I signed those divorce papers.. Her last name is still Swan-Mills so that makes her my wife and last but not lease.. Who said the kid she's carrying is yours?"

"Excuse me?"

"(Laughs) You heard me."

"What is she talking about Regina?" He glares at her.

"I'm talking about the time I came over to check on my kids but they weren't there and we got to talking about old times and she told me that she hasn't had an orgasm since I fucked her sooooooo.. I took care of it.. I fucked her like she's suppose to be fucked.. Unlike you.. What?? You last about 2 or 3 minutes and then you're done??? (Laughs) I fuck her until she passes out.. Now how about you go back to whatever hole you crawled out of and take your hands off my wife or I will shot you."

"You bitch." She says and he slaps Regina across the face and I lost it..

GUN SHOTS

Screams

"Help me." A lady yells.

"Fuck Emma are you okay?" I hear Regina ask.. "EMMA! EMMA!! Help me somebody please!!! I need Help!! Emma can you hear me?? EMMA!"

CHAPTER 13

"Sorry Regina.. Yeah I heard you, is he dead?" I ask.

"No Emma but you did shoot him.."

"I should have killed him."

"Emma calm down." Regina says.

"Has he hit you before?" I ask.

"Now is not the time nor the place."

"Fine.. Lets go."

"Can you let me know when he is out of surgery?" Regina asks.

"Yes Madam Mayor." The doctor says.

"Thank you."

"Yes mama."

"Now Emma we.."

"Let's go Regina.. My place or yours?"

"Yours is fine."

———————— My Place —————-

"Why didn't you tell me he beats you?" I ask.

"Emma you were happy and you had a baby on the way and I didn't want to come in between you and Gabby."

"Regina you are the mother of my two kids I will always be there for you and don't ever think you are coming between anything because when it comes to you or our kids you all comes first.. No matter what.. You and our two kids will..."

"Three." She whispers.

"Excuse me?"

"Three kids."

"Regina what are you talking about?" I ask standing up from the couch.

"It's your baby." She says just above a whisper.

"Are you serious?"

"Yes.."

"Why the fuck didn't you tell me?"

"Because you moved on and you looked happy with Gabby and,.."

"Regina I don't care if I looked happy.. You're pregnant with my kid and you didn't tell me."

"I'm sorry." She says and a tear falls down her cheek.

"Fuck.. Baby I didn't mean to make you cry.. I'm sorry." I say.

"No I'm the one who is sorry.. I just didn't want to ruin your happi ness.."

"Without you I am never happy."

"But Gabby."

"Yes I loved Gabby.. But it was different with her than it was with you."

"I know.. I bet it was less stressful huh?"

"Hey I didn't say that."

"I know.. But I also know I can be a pain In The ass sometimes."

"That's what I love the most about you.. And I still do.. Love you I mean.. Yeah.. I love you."

"I love you too." She says and I lean in to kiss her.. Damn it feels good to kiss her again. "I miss your kisses." She whispers.

"I miss yours too." I whisper against her neck and that's when I heard her breath hiss.. So of course I go to kissing on her..

"(Moans) Emma." She Moans.

"I'm happy your pregnant, but I hate I can't fuck you the way I want to."

"And what way is that?" She asks.

"So hard that you won't remember the pain that has torn us apart."

"I promise I won't stop you."

"I can't fuck you like that when you're pregnant Gina."

"I'm almost 7 months pregnant and I can handle you Papi." She whispers against my lip.

"Mmmmm.. Regina." I say and she pulls me by my belt buckle so that I'm closer to her.. "(Gasps) Regina wait a second we don't.."

"This is happening Emma." She undo my belt and unzip my pants. "I'm going to make you feel so good.. You remember how I used to wake you up from a stressful night?" She asks and now she has her hand around me.. "I kind of remember it going something like this." And without another word she took me in her mouth..

"(Moans) Ah!! Fuck Mmmmm.. (Gasps) Slow baby.. Gina I'm.." She ignore me just like she always do.. "Mmmmm... Fuck!! Ah!! Gina.. I fucking love you.." I say and she makes eye contact with me before she takes me deeper into her mouth. "Holy Shit." Her eyes are rolling to the back of her head. "Just like that baby.. Don't stop.. Just like that." I grab a fist full of her hair when I start to feel myself climax and that's when lost it.. I held her head tight while I fucked her mouth.. "(Moans) Ah!!! Ahhhh!!! Open your eyes.. Look at me.." I whisper and she does.. That's all I needed to push me over the edge.. "I'm coming.. Ah!! Ahh! (Passionate Screams) Fuck!! (Panting) I'm sorry." I say looking down at her and she just grabs around of me and lick me clean. "You're a naughty young lady."

"Only for you.. You still taste good."

"And you still give amazingly mind blowing head."

"Thank you."

"No... Thank you Gina." She just smiles at me while she sticks her hand in her panties.. It's easy access because she has on a dress. "Stop.. what are you doing?" I ask.

"I'm so wet.. I feel like I've wet my pants." She says and I instantly get hard again.. "(Moans) I can hear how wet I am.. Listen.." She says and she pumps her fingers harder... "Ah.... You hear that.. (Gasps) Nobody makes me this wet.. Only you."

"Regina."

"(Moans) Come taste me." Whisper and her head falls back and her back arches off the couch.. I know she is about to come so before that happens I move her hand and dive right in.. Sucking her clit and licking her folds all at once.. "(Moans) Ahh!! Emma!! I'm coming.. Ah!!!! (Gasps) Mmmm.. (panting)." Her body is like jelly now..

"You okay?"

"(Panting) I'm fine.. Thank you.." She whispers before she lay down.

"(Laughs) Are you tired?" I ask her.

"Very.. I'm taking a nap."

"Okay baby.. I'll be here when you get up." I say before I walk away to head upstairs.

"Hey Em??"

"Yeah Baby?"

"I love you."

"I love you too Gina.. Get some rest." I lean down and give her kiss.

"Yes Papi:"

CHAPTER 14

"We need to get up before the kids get up." I whisper in her ear.

"Emma I'm tired." She says.

"Regina we've slept all yesterday and it's 11am."

"Yeah well you fucked me to good and now I'm tired."

"If you don't get up I'm.."

"Please do." She turned around and got on top of me.

"You didn't let me finish." I say.

"You're hard.. Do I turn you on Miss Swan?" Before I answer I flip her over so that I'm on top.

"I told you that's not my name.. It's Swan-Mills.. And don't you ever forget that Madam Mayor."

"And if I forget again?"

"I'll fuck you so hard that it will be impossible for you to walk for a year."

"I'm so wet from you saying that."

"Well you'll be wet for a few hours because Sam is up and we need to talk to them."

"Fine.. You go start breakfast and I'll go get myself off." She whispers in my ear.

"Only if you think about me."

"What??? You're going to let me get myself off?"

"Only if you can except the challenge."

"(Laughs) Yeah right."

"I'll be down stairs Gina." I say smiling at her.

———————-

"Good morning mom." Sam says.

"Morning baby."

"I came over here because ma didn't come home last night.. But if I would have known you and Gabby was going to be going at it like animals then I would have stayed at home."

"About that.." Regina says.

"No fucking way."

"Watch your mouth young lady." Regina says.

"So you're telling me you and mama was upstairs banging each other?" Sam asks.

"Banging??? Who says banging?" Regina asks.

"Well Fucking.. I was trying to watch my language but yeah.. You two were up there fucking..."

"Sam stop with the fuck work please." I say.

"Mama said it so many times and now that I think about it.. I'm going to be sick.. Excuse me but I think I'm going out for breakfast." Sam says.

"Samantha you are having breakfast with us.. Your brother is in his way now and."

"Hey mom.. Oh hey Mama.. I didn't know you were coming." Henry says.

"Oh she already did." Sam whispers.

"SAMANTHA!!" Regina yells..

"I'm sorry.. I'm confused.. And mama why are you here?"

"Let's just say she was here long before we got here."

"You didn't come home last night and if you were here when Sam got here last night.. Then that means you stayed the night and if you stayed the night that means you and mom.. (Gasps) You were total banging last night." Henry smiles at us.

"Stop with the banging word please." Regina says.

"Well fucking.. Were two were fucking each other and thought you could hide it."

"Okay if one of you say something else I don't like, I'm going to bury you."

"So are you two back together?" Sam asks.

"I don't know because we.."

"Yes we are back together.. Now what's for breakfast we are hungry... And by we I mean me and my baby."

"(Gasps) You can have sex this close to giving birth?" Henry asks.

"What did I just say?" Regina says.

"Sorry.." He says.

"And yes.. Now drop it."

"One more question." Sam asks.

"What is it?" Regina asks.

"How is this going to work with you carrying Robin's kid?"

"Oh about that.. It's my kid and he can go to hell." I say.

"(Laughs) Mom you can't take his kid.. He's a really mean jerk he will try and take us to court and everything.. What if he.. Never mind.. Sorry mama I won't say anything."

"It's okay.. She knows."

"That he ugh.."

"Yes.. Your mother knows that Robin hits me."

"I'm sorry what?" Sam says.

"Sam it's okay now.. I'm."

"He put his hands on you and you didn't say anything?"

"Henry walked in on him when he slapped me in the face and pushed me down on the bed."

"That some of bitch."

"Samantha language." Regina says.

"Fuck that.. He hit you and you didn't say anything.. Mom do something." Samantha says.

"I did.. I shot him.. Now who wants bacon?" I said.

"You shot him?" Henry says.

"Yes."

"If I had a gun I would have killed him.. I tried to fight him off but he was way stronger than me.. He broke my arm and crushed my ankle with his steel toe work boots." And that pissed me off.

"Regina the kids will finish breakfast for you.. I'll be back later."

"Emma wait.. Where are you going?"

"To do what I should have done in the first place." I say grabbing my truck keys.

"Emma you are not going to go and kill him." Regina says.

"He put his fucking hands on my kid!" I yell..

"Please calm down."

"I was pissed when I found out what he did to you Gina and that's why I shot him.. But to know that he was the cause of my kid's scholarship.. He broke his arm and crushed his angle Regina.. You know he's a dead man."

"Emma you've changed.. Please don't do this.. Your daughter needs you." She says.

"Regina.. Baby .. I'm.."

"Please think about the baby.. He is not worth it."

"Fine.. But if he shows his face around you or my kids.. I'm putting a bullet in his head." I then walk out the door.

———————————————————————————————

———————

CHAPTER 15

"**W**here have you been?" Regina asks me.

"Out.. I just had to clear my head."

"Oh.."

"It's not like that.. I was angry and upset okay.. I'm sorry."

"How are you feeling?" She asks.

"I'm fine Gina.. How are you?"

"I didn't lose a baby.. You did and I'm worried about you because you haven't had time to process it.. And by trying to distract me with sex earlier today is not going to help.. So answer my question.. How are you."

"Fine." I then walk away.

"Stop it." She whispers.

"Regina I can't talk about it right now."

"Right.. So you're going to drink your problems away like before?"

"Don't do that.. Don't.."

"Emma this is not healthy and I'll be damned if I watched you throw your life away.. I know you're in pain baby.. Please.. Please don't take it out with Anger in the wrong way.."

"You mean like lightning Robin up like a Christmas Tree!" I yell and it scared her.. "I'm sorry."

"What's going on?" Henry asks.

"We're going to my house for a few days.."

"Are you two fighting?"

"No we were talking Henry.. Go back to bed."

"No you were yelling." He says.

"Go pack a bag and Wake up your sister."

"Regina please stop."

"I'm not staying here and you.."

Knock Knock

"Regina I know you're in here." Someone yells at the door and I can't believe it.. It's Robin.

"Oh he got balls showing up at my house." I say grabbing my gun.

"Emma no.. Don't do this."

"Open the door Bitch."

"Regina get out of my way."

"Put the gun down.. You are not going to shoot him." She says and I walk pass her and open the door.

"I know she's in there now move." He demands me.

"You got some balls coming here?" I say.

"Regina get your ass out here right now." He says.

"You got less than a second to get off of my property before I shoot you. And this time it will definitely be a kill shot." And her just looks at me so I point the gun to his head. "One... Two.."

"Emma please stop." Regina comes and put her hand on my shoulder.

"Bitch let's go." Robin says.

"Call her another bitch and I will shoot you."

"What's going on?" Henry asks.

"Nothing.. Go back to bed." I say.

"Oh look there is your bitch of a son too." He says and that was it.. I lost it.

—-Gun Shoots —-

"Ahhh!!! You fucking shot me." He yelled.

"Emma!" Regina yells at me.

Sirens

"Boss what's going on?" One of my officers ask.

"Nothing.. Get this trash off my property." I say.

"Pack your bags because we are leaving." I hear Regina tell the kids.

"Regina don't do this.." I say.

"Your behavior is out of hand and you're.."

"I HAVE MY REASONS REGINA!!" I yell.

"And I have mine."

"I'm.. I'm sorry for yelling."

"Mom maybe we can come back in the morn for breakfast when you've calmed down." Samantha says with tears in her eyes.

"Sweetheart I'm.."

"We love you mom.. Let's talk in morning for breakfast okay."

"Okay.. I love you.. Hey kid take care of your ma and sister okay."

"Okay ma.. love you."

"Love you to kid.."

"Emma.." Regina says.

"Baby.. I'm sorry."

"I know and I love you.. We'll talk in the morning."

"Yeah.. Love you more." I say and she smiles.

"Not possible." She smiles back before she leaves.. Once the door close I broke down crying.

"(Screams) Fuck!!!"

The Next Day

"I wake up to the smell of bacon." And that put a smile on my face..

"Morning." I look over to see Regina drinking a cup of water.

"Morning beautiful."

"How are you?" She asks.

"Better.. Look Gina I'm sorry about last night.. And I'm so so sorry I yelled at you." I say with tears in my ears.

"I know baby.. But please go see someone.. You lost your baby and the woman you loved so I think that will help."

"I will."

"Get dressed and meet us in the kitchen."

"Yes ma'am."

"Morning my babies." I say to Sam and Henry.

"Morning mom.. Breakfast is ready."

"It smells good."

"Thank you." Henry says and we all sit down.

"Hey mom.. Ma said you had to tell us something."

"Yeah uh.. There is no easy way to say this."

"Are you okay."

"No.. But I will be.. But uhh.. Gabby was in an accident."

"Is she okay?? Is the baby okay?? Did she have the baby?? Where are they?" Sam asked standing up.

"Sit down baby." I whisper.

"No.. Let's go see Gabby.. Where is she?"

"She's gone."

"What!! Gone?!! Gone where?"

"She left town."

"What about the baby?" Henry asked.

"The baby uh... She.."

"She didn't make it." Regina finished my sentence when she notice I couldn't get it out.

"Wha.. What?" Sam ask and I can tell she was about to cry.

"There complications and the baby.. Well she didn't make it."

"It was a girl?" Henry asked.

"Yes."

"I'm sorry mom." Sam says.

"Thank you baby.. But I'm okay.. Well I'm not okay but I will be.. As long as your mother doesn't leave me again." I say smiling at her.

"I'll always love you mi amor and I'll never leave you again." She stands up and kiss me.

"Okay that's enough." He says.

"Yeah.. Because we do not was to here you guys banging later on."

"Stop saying banging." Regina says.

"Well you said don't say fuck.. Soo."

"Don't say that either!"

"Well don't have sex while we're in the house."

"Deal." I say looking at Regina.

"I have a lot of questions about what really happen Ed with Gabby and the driver but I'll wait until everything die down." Henry said..

"No you can ask me now." I say.

"No because you're going through enough right now so... Yeah I'll wait."

"Okay."

"Soooo.. I have a date tonight." Sam says.

CHAPTER 16

"(Moans) Don't stop." The way Regina is moaning in my ear is sending waves of chills down my spine. "Ahhhhh that feels so good."

"You feel amazing."

"Fuck me harder Emma." Regina grabs me by my throat to let me know she is serious but how could I do that when she's almost ready to pop.

"Mmmm.. Baby I.."

"Now!! Emma." She throws her head back into the mattress and her Moans got louder to the second.. "Show me how much you really love me." She whispered against my lips...

Fuck It !!

"(Moans) Are you ready?" I ask.. Because who am I to reject Regina when she clearly stated that she is okay.

"Don't ask me just (GASPS) oh.... my.... godddddd.." She screamed when I started pounding my way inside her not thinking about the fact that she is pregnant and how dangers it might be.. "Oh baby.. You fuck me so good."

"Who's pussy is this?" I ask with a smirk on my face.

"Yours.. Always have been and always will be."

"That's my girl.." I kiss her and go back to pounding inside her. I know she's about to come because her hand went around my throat and started to squeeze.. "That's it baby.. Give it to me." I say.

"I'm coming." She whisper before her eyes disappeared to the back of her head. "Ooohhhhh Yesssssss (Gasps) Don't stop baby.. Don't stop!!!! Keep fucking me." Her legs started to Shake underneath me and her nails clawed into my back.

"Ahh!!! Fuck Gina.. I'm coming." I yell.

"Mmmmm.. I love watching you come undone." Regina whisper.

"I love watching you to baby." I say rolling over to the other side of the bed. "Are you hungry?" I ask.

"Yes.. You wanna start breakfast and I'll be down in a few minutes?" She asks.

"Yeah.. Sure just let me go clean myself up and I'll head down there."

"Mmmmhmmm.." she hummms. And I know she's about to go to sleep.

"Gina.. You better not go to sleep." I laugh.

"I promise I'm not.. I'm just resting my eyes."

"Bull Shit. (Laughs) You're falling asleep."

"Baby please just give me like 30 minutes and I'll be down okay.. You fucked me to good and now I'm tired."

"You're lucky I love you." I whisper in her and she's sound asleep that fast. "I can't wait til marry you again." I smile down at her.

————————————Breakfast ——————————

"Where is mama?" Samantha asks.

"She's taking a nap." I say telling her to keep it down.

"At 10am?? She's never slept in this long."

"She's ughhh.. Tired.. You know with the pregnancy and all.."

"Or maybe because you too were banging all night." Henry says.

"Henry Daniel Swan-Mills stop saying banging." I turn to see Regina coming down the stairs.

"Baby what did I say about coming down the stairs on this side.. It's to many walk down with you being pregnant.. Why didn't you come down on the other side?" I ask with a concerned look on my face.

"Because I wanted to see how you would react?" She smiles.

"Congratulations I'm pissed." I say walking away.

"Emma wait I was joking."

"You could seriously get hurt coming down there and then what?" I ask.

"I'm sorry baby.. I will not come back down on this side until I have the baby and I'm all healed up."

"You promise?" I ask.

"I promise and I also promise I'll make it up to you tonight." She says with a smile on her face.

"Ewwww.. Don't tell me you are going to be fucking all night again."

"SAMANTHA!" I yell.

"Sorry.. And Mom I'm going to take a breakfast Togo.. My ride is outside." Sam says.

"Who's taking you?" I ask.

"Just a friend." She replied back.

"Or maybe your boyfriend." Henry says.

"Excuse me?" Regina says.

"Thanks a lot Jack ass." Sam says.

"HEY!! Language.. Sam what boyfriend?" I ask.

"He just started college and.."

"Oh hell no." Regina says walking to the front door.

"What are you doing ma?" Sam asks.

"I want to meet this boyfriend of yours."

"Mom tell her no please." Sam asks.

"Baby it's okay you don't have to go outside and meet him.. It's fine." I say walking over to Regina.

"Thanks mom."

"I'll go meet him." I say opening the door.

"WHAT!!! No!!!"

"Hello could you step out of the vehicle please." I say.

"Oh ugh.. Sure." He steps out the car and throws down a cigarette... And he has failed already. "What's up." And that is no way to talk to the parent of the girl you like.

"Tyler I'm so sorry." Sam says.

"All good baby.. is this your mother?" He asks her.

"I am and this is her other mother Regina."

"Damn so you're like... You know?" He asks with a smile on his face.

"Like what?" Henry asks.

"Henry calm down."

"Oh I have no problem with it.. I think it's hot actually.. And you two are very fine by the way.. I see where Sam gets it from.."

"Oh my god Tyler stop talking."

"I don't think I want my sister dating a dumb ass want a be bad boy who thinks it's cool to tell his girlfriend's parents that it's hot that they are lesbians."

"I'm sorry dude I was just saying that maybe..."

"Maybe what?" Henry says walking up to his face.

"Nothing.. I was just saying that.."

"Well I'm saying get back in your car and drive away before I make you wish your mom kept her legs close and you were never born."

"Henry that's enough go back in side sweetheart." Regina says.

"Thanks Henry." Sam says.

"Baby let's go." Tyler says.

"I think I'm riding with my brother."

"I drove all this fucking way and you decide you don't want a ride?" He yells.

"Hey watch your tone with my daughter." I say.

"And if I don't?" He says with a smile.

Best Day Ever I think to my self............

"Thank you." I say with a smile.

"For what?" He asks. And I pull my handcuffs from my pockets..

"Because you just made my day.. Turn around?"

"What??? You're going to try and arrest me?" He smiles.

"Try??? Oh I am."

"Good luck." He says before grabs Sam by her arm.

"HEY!!" She yells and kicks him in the balls.. "That hurt my arm."

"That's my girl." Regina says.

"You bitch." He says.

"And you're a low life disrespect little boy."

"Oh there is nothing little about me at all.. Ask your daughter." He says laughing.

"Get up." I grab him by his arm and put the hand cuffs on him. "You're under arrest and you have the right to remain silent so shut the hell up."

"One smile from me and I had your daughter head over hills for me.. Isn't that right Samantha?"

"Fuck you Tyler." Sam whisper and the look on Regina's face shows sad and anger.

"Been there done that... Or should I say I already have."

"I hate you and we're done."

"Baby please don't go.. I'm going to miss that pretty little mouth of yours." He smiles. "Ahhhh!!!! Fuck!" He yells after I tighten the cuffs.

"What's wrong?? Did it hurt??" I ask.

"You bitch." He says and I tighten it again. "Ahhh!!"

"Say it again." I say and he just looks at me.. "Thought so.. Now let's go.. Sorry baby you have to tell Henry to finish breakfast.. I have a bonus to go collect."

"Bonus?" Tyler asks.

"Shut up." I throw him in the back seat and walk over to Regina. "I love you baby and I'll see you on my lunch break." I kiss her goodbye.

"I love you too baby." She kisses me back and walks in the house.

CHAPTER 17

"Samantha sweetheart we need to talk." Regina says.

"I want to be alone mama." She whispers.

"I know baby but we need to talk." I say.

"Fine." She says and Regina opens the door.

"Sweetheart are you okay?" Regina asks Sam.

"No mom.. My boyfriend who I thought loved me, embarrassed me in front of you guys so no.. I'm not okay."

"Honey I don't care about that but I do want to talk about is what he said."

"Which part?" Sam asks.

"Ughh.. When he ugh.." I struggled to say it.

"How long have you been sexual active?" Regina says.

"Oh god.." Samantha covers her face.

"No that long okay.. I see now that it was a mistake.. All he care about it is... Nevermind."

"You say what's on your mind sweetheart." Regina says.

"You calling me sweetheart makes it sound like you feel sorry for me."

"It's not that we feel sorry for you honey.. We.."

"And you mom.. What's with the honey?"

"Okay Samantha listen.. You we're having sex with this boy and tell us about." Regina says.

"Oh and now she's pissed.. Now that's the mama I know."

"Well I'm Pregnant and under a lot of pressure so forgive me if I'm being a little polite about it."

"I didn't you guys because I didn't think I had to."

"Excuse me?? You didn't have to." I say.

"Yeah.. Henry has been fucking those cheerleaders for years and you haven't been questioning him.. Have you??

"HENRY!" Regina yells.

"Oh crap! No mama wait I didn't mean.."

"Oh no I heard what you said."

"Ma'am?" Henry says walking into the room.

"So you're having sex too." Regina asks. And Henry eyes went wide.

"You rat!!!" He yells.

"Answer me." Regina whispers.

"Yes ma but I'm careful I swear."

"Are you careful with all of them?" I ask.

"Dang Samantha you told her about the threesome too? What else did you tell them because.."

"Henry wait.." Samantha tries to cut in but it's too late.

"You had a threesome?? Are you fucking serious?" Regina yells.

"Look baby maybe you shouldn't be yelling so much considering you're.."

"Don't tell me what to do Miss Swan."

"Call me Miss Swan again and I'll take you to our bedroom." I whisper in her ear and she was lost for words.

"Jesus Christ mom what did you say to her??? She looks like she's about to pass out." Sam asks.

"Nothing that concerns you and Henry?? A threesome really?" I ask with a smile.

"Emma I swear to god if you are smiling about this I will break you.."

"Right ugh.. Son that's not cool.. You could easily catch a disease you should be more careful."

"I used a condom.. I'm not stupid and I only did it with one of them.. The other chick was.. Nevermind let's just say she was a little occupied at the time I was banging the other chick if you know what I mean." He says with a smile.

"Stop smiling before I slap it off your face.. Go to you room.. This conversation is not over."

"Yes ma'am." He says before he walks out..

"And you.. We are going to the clinic in the morning to get you tested and then I'm putting you on.. (Gasps) Fuck." Regina whispers.

"What is it baby?" I ask.

"Nothing.. What I was says was Tomorrow I'm putting you on birth control because I'm.. (Screams) FUCK!!" She yells.

"Regina what is happening?" I ask for the second time.

"I'm fine."

"Please don't lie to me right now."

"I think we should go the hospital."

"Why?? Are you?? Oh god?? The baby is coming isn't it?"

"I think so."

"HENRY!" I yell.

"Mom it won't happen again I promise and I'll be sure to tell you guys if I.."

"We will worry about that later.. Go crank up the car your mother is in labor."

"Wait.. Now?? You mean the baby is.."

"Yes dumb ass the baby is coming." Sam says.

"Language Samantha!" Regina says.

"Try not to tell baby.. Calm down."

"Calm down for what?? You did this to me.."

"I know and I'm sorry."

"Yeah me too because we are never having sex again."

"Gina baby I'm.. Wait what?"

"(Laughs)." Samantha is laughing.

"Go get your mother bag since you think everything is so funny." I say.

"Okay."

"The car is ready.. Let's go." Henry says.

"Regina can you walk?"

"A little yeah.."

"Put your arm around me.. I'll carry you."

"I can walk." She says.

"I said I'm carrying you." I say picking her up.

———-At The Hospital————

"Yes ummm.. I need a doctor my wife is in labor." I say carrying her inside..

"I need some help over here." the lady yells.

"Thank you."

"Lay her down please." She says.

"Yeah sure.. Umm could you do something for the pain please?" I ask.

"We'll take good care of her." The lady says and she winks at me.

"I will kill." Regina says.

"Oh I'm.. (Clears Throat) Sorry.. I was just.."

"Eye fucking my wife?" Regina says.

"No ma'am."

"Can someone get me a doctor who is not high on hormones.. And someone who doesn't want to fuck my wife!" She yells.

"I'll help." A man comes by smiling.

"Yes you can." Regina says.

"Get lost." I say.

"EMMA!" Regina yells.

"You really think I'm going to let him deliver our daughter??? He thinks you're attractive and now he gets the privilege to see your pussy.. I'm sorry I mean Vagina.. Yeah.. Over my dead body.. Hey you??? Are you a doctor?" I ask the older lady at the desk who was filling out some papers.

"Yes why?"

"My wife is in labor being everyone is so fixated on how good we look they can't seem to do their job... Can you do it?"

"Yes I can.. Right this way people.. We have a baby to deliver.."

"Best things I've heard all night.." We get in the room and Regina starts to scream.

"(Screams) Ahhhh!!! Fuck!!!! Get her out of me now!!!!" Regina yells. And the doctor tells her to push once we were all in the room.. We asked if Henry and Sam could join us..

"Okay Regina.. Push."

"(Screams) Fuck!!! No more after this Emma.. You hear me??!" She yells and the doctor tells her to push again.

"Okay again.. Push."

"I love you baby." I whisper in her ear.

"One last push Regina.. You are doing great."

"Ahhhh!!!! (Panting) No more." She says.

"(Baby Crying)!"

"Congratulations you have a baby girl." The woman says.

"Wow she looks like you mom.." Henry says.

"That's crazy.." Samantha says.

"What is honey?" Regina asks.

"Nothing.. It's just I look like you and she looks like mom.."

"Yeah.. Probably because your mom did this to me on purpose."

"I did not."

"Oh she is biologically yours?" The doctor says.

"Yeah.. I was born intersex." I say..

"Oh you.. You umm.. Have a ummm... (Clears Throat) You have a penis?" She asks.

"She does." Regina answers.

"Wow that's very I'm.. Wow." She says looking at the front of my pants.

"Eyes up here doctor." Regina says.

"Right sorry.. I'll leave you too it." She smiles and I smile back.

"Keep smiling and I'll break it." I heard Regina say..

"Sorry." I say.

"Emma get the baby I don't feel too good."

"Wait what's happening?" I ask.

Beep Beep

"Henry get a doctor now!" I yell. "Baby??"

"Emma I'm.." Regina started to say something but she couldn't finish before she passed out..

"Baby?? Regina!! REGINA!" I yell.

CHAPTER 18

"What's wrong with her?" I ask.

"I need you all to leave the room please." The lady says as she walk Henry and Sam out of the room. "Emma you too."

"Hell no.. You fix my wife."

"I can't do that with you in here screaming in my ear now I ask again.. Please leave."

"She's coming back." The other doctor says.

"Regina??? Gina Baby?" I say and I get no answer.

"She can't hear you."

"WHAT!" I yell.

"She can't hear because she is out cold.. She's alive but she needs plenty of rest.."

"You just said she was waking up and I'm staying with her."

"Take your children to get something to eat and visit the nursery.. Come back in a couple of hours." He says.

"Hey you.." I point to the nurse. "Look lady you call me if anything changes.. I don't care if her heart drops or if it stays the same.. You call me.. As a matter of fact.. Call me every 30 minutes to an hour or I'll hunt you down.. Understood??"

"Yeah.. Yes ma'am.. Yeah.. Crystal."

"Thank you." I say handing her my daughter.

"Em.. Emma." Regina says..

"Hey.. Hey baby I'm right here."

"Don't leave me."

"I'm not going anywhere.. You get some rest okay.. we'll be here when you wake up."

"You.. You promise?"

"I promise... And Gina?"

"Yeah.."

"I love you."

"I love you too.. And stay away from her." She says looking at the nurse that was checking me out earlier.

"(Laughs) I only got eyes for you my love.. Now rest."

"Okay.. I'll cut it Emma.. Don't temp me again." And with that she fell asleep.

"Ooookkkayyy.. I see she's the same old Regina." I say walking out the door.

————————————

"Is mama okay?" Sam ask and I can tell she has been crying.

"Yeah.. She's okay."

"It didn't look like it."

"Hey.. Your mama is strong and she will be okay."

"But mom..."

"Samantha listen to me.. Your mama is okay.. She was just talking to me."

"So she did wake up?"

"Yes sweetheart."

"Oh.. okay.."

"Where is Henry?"

"He got angry and punch the windows out over there and the police took him outside.. I tried to go but he told me to wait here."

"Okay.. Take my bank card go get us some food and come right back."

"Okay."

"Are you okay to drive?"

"Yeah mom.. I promise."

"Okay.. I have to go get your brother.. Be careful.. I love you."

"I love you too mom."

————————————————

"Hey office I can take it from here."

"Hey boss."

"Hey Jack.. Thank you for taking him."

"Of course.. He's upset I brought him out to get some air."

"Thank you."

"Come on Henry."

"I don't want to go back in there."

"Well I'll be sure to tell your mama that you didn't want to come see her."

"Wait.. She's okay?"

"Yes."

"But the monitor was going off and she passed out.. She.. She.."

"Hey your mama is fine.. She woke up and called my name and I told her to get some rest."

"Holly shit mom.. I total lost it in there.. I think I scared the other kids.."

"It's okay my son.."

"I'm sorry mom."

"Let's go wait inside for your sister to come back."

"Okay."

————————

"Your wife is doing good. She's being asking for you but everytime we come and get you she's already back asleep but your daughter is doing great.. You may go upstairs and hold her if you like.. We'll get your wife moved out of the icu and into a family room.. I'm sure you and your other children would like to stay with her."

"Yes doctor.. Thank you.."

"You're welcome Emma.. (Clears Throat) Sorry.. I mean Mrs. Swan-Mills."

"Yeah.. Well I'll go get the kids and take them to see their sister.. I'll meet you guys in Regina's room.. Thanks."

"You're more than welcome." She smiles and wink at me before she walks away..

"Mama is going to kill you." Sam says.

"I wasn't flirting with her."

"I know.. But mama will kill you if you look at another woman."

"I only have eyes for your mother."

"Oh I know it."

"Good.. Now text your brother and tell him to meet us upstairs so we can see your sister."

"Deal."

———————————- One Hour Later ———————————-

"Em.. Em-ma." I hear Regina say.

"Baby.. Hey.. Hey.. Are you okay?" I say with tears in my eyes.

"I'm fine.. Why are you crying?"

"I thought I would never see you again."

"Why would you think that?"

"Your heart stopped and....."

"Wait what??"

"I'm sorry.. I.. Oh baby.. I love so much!!! Please don't ever think I don't okay?"

"Emma I'm okay baby.. I promise.. And I love you too.." And she gives me that beautiful smile I love to see. "Where are my babies?"

"Sam is sleeping and Henry is over there with the baby... He flip out earlier and one of my officers escorted him out."

"Henry.. Sweetheart come here."

"Mama.. Are.. Are you okay? Do you need anything?? I'll go get the doctors."

"Henry wait baby please come here and sit down."

"But mama you.."

"Come here." As he walks over He takes his head phones out and sit next to his mother.

"I'm glad you're okay ma."

"I'm not going anywhere."

"When those machines went out and you stopped breathing.. Mom was calling for you and you didn't move and then they.. They.. (Crying) They started.."

"Hey !! Hey!! I'm fine now.. And I'm so sorry you had to see that.. I'm sorry you and your sister had to go through that." Seeing Regina cry like that broke my heart. "And I promise I'll do my best not to scare you guys like that again."

"Ma?? Are you okay?" Sam wakes up and say.

"I'm fine baby."

"But earlier you.. You.. Wait why are you crying??? Mom call the doctor... HELP!!" Sam yells.

"Samantha baby.. Calm down I'm fine okay.. I promise and I'm sorry I scared you earlier.. I never wanted you guys to experience something like that.."

"Everything okay in here Emma?" The nurse ask and it had to be her.

"Oh.. So you too are on first name basis??"

"(Laughs) Gina baby.. It's not like that."

"It better not be.. Because I meant what I said!!! I will cut it off."

"I.. (Clears Throat) I believe you my love."

"Good.. Now be a good Wife and please get your wife something to drink."

"Yes ma'am."

"I would like to monitor you a few more extra days before your release date.. I would like to keep an eye on you before you leave."

"Me or my wife?" Regina asks.

"Oh shit!!! Fuck!" I whisper.

"Just you ma'am." The nurse smiles at Regina and I'm scared shitless!!!

"Good to know.. You my leave now.. I would like some privacy with my "WIFE" and my children.."

"Yes ma'am.. Have a good night.."

"Oh I will." Regina says before she shuts the door. "If that bitch try you one more time I will find a way to get out this bed and break her face.. And why the fuck does she keep smiling for??"

"I think ma is back to her normal." Sam whispered.

"Yeah me too... Sam let's go get something to eat and let them talk."

"Sure.. Love you guys." Sam says..

"We love you both too.." I say before they shut the door..

"Hi." She smiles at me.

"Hey baby."

"Kiss me."

"(Laughs) No.. Now gets some rest."

"You're no fun."

"Whatever.. But for real baby.. Rest.. I love you and I'll be right here when you wake up.."

"Okay baby.." I kissed her forehead and told her rest.

CHAPTER 19

"It's good to have you home baby." I say.

"It's good to be home." She pulls me down and kiss me. "I can't wait to heal."

"Why baby?? What's wrong?? Are you hurting?" I ask.

"Only my ego."

"(Laughs) Baby what are you talking about?"

"I miss the way you fuck me.. I can't wait for you to do it again."

"Ewww.. I was coming up here to ask you guys what you wanted for Dinner but nevermind.. I lost my appetite." Sam says.

"I'm sorry baby.. You mother is on a lot of medication.. She's not going to be herself for a few days." I say.

"I'm fine thank you.. I just miss my wife making passionate rough love to me."

"I've heard enough.. Mom I'm eating out with my friends." Sam says.

"You see what you've done Regina?? You ran our daughter off."

"Good.. I wanted you to do something for me."

"Anything for you my love."

"Take off your pants and come lay down."

"(Clears Throat) What?" I whisper.

"Do it.. I'm not trying to get you to fuck me.. I know we can't.. Just do it and come lay down next me." She says and I do as I'm told. "God I love you Emma."

"Are you saying that because I'm half naked with only my boxes and sports bra on?"

"No.. I mean you do have a sexy ass body, but that's not why I love you.. You know why I love you."

"I do.." I say and she cuddle close to me.

"If you wanted to cuddle with me all you had to do was ask.. You didn't have to make me strip out of my clothes."

"I wanted you half naked for a reason baby." And then I noticed her running her fingers up and down my abs..

"Baby.. (Laughs) Stop.. Don't get me excited when you know I can't.. (Gasps) Fuck!" She grabs me between my legs..

"I can get you excited whenever I want.."

"I know baby but now is not.. Mmmmm it's not the best time."

"Why is that?" She kisses my neck and then my chest.. After that she looks at me and smile before she kisses my stomach..

"Baby stop.. I can wait until you heal.."

"Wait for what?" She asks. And before I could answer her question my boxers were ripped from my body within seconds.

"Regina (Laughs) Baby.."

"Sit up and sit on the edge of the bed."

"(Laughs) Are you okay?" I ask.

"I will be when you so kindly do as I ask."

"You better be glad I love you woman." I lean over and sit at the edge of the bed and Regina gets on her knees in front of me.

"Mmm.. I love you too." She leans down and takes me in her mouth..

"(Gasps) Mmmm.. Fuck!" I move her hair out of the way so I could see her eyes.. "Just like that baby.. Mmmm.. You know just what I like.. (Moans) Ahh!!!"

————— Front Door Opens Then Closes ———-

"Gina baby.." I say but she just pushes me deeper into her mouth.. "Holy Shit!" I whisper..

"Mom!" Henry yells.

"Ah!!! Fuck!!! Ugh Henry put the groceries up please I.. (Moans) Damn baby.."

"What did you say?" Henry asks.

"Put up the groceries!" I yell. "Baby.. I'm close.. I'm.. Ah.." She just goes faster and deeper.. It's like she's lost in her own world.. At one point I don't even think she heard Henry come in the front door.. Or us talking..

"Mom I can't hear you I'm coming up stairs."

"Fuck!! Regina stop.. Henry is.." And she squeezed my balls.. "Ahh!! Fuck!!" And that's when I came in her mouth..

"Mom what were you saying because I.. Oh my god!!" Henry turns around and yells.. "what the fuck you guys?"

"Shit!" I yell grabbing the covers to cover up myself and Regina wipes her mouth before she turns around to get up and sit down next to me..

"Henry language.. It's not like you don't have those girls at school on their knees.."

"How about you guys lock the door next time." Henry says.

"I didn't have time." Regina says.

"Don't you have to like wait a little before you know.. All of this."

"Henry I gave your mom head.. It's natural.. She wasn't going to fuck me.. I wanted to give her something special before dinner because my medicine is going to put me to sleep soon.. So.. Be a good boy and put up the groceries like your mom asked."

"Gladly.." He says slamming the door.

"Dramatic much!" Regina yells.

"You are out of control woman." I say to her.

"Just wait until I'm all healed up.. I am going to fuck you like my life depends on it.."

"I can't wait to fuck you too.. You've been very disobedient.."

"I'll be sure to be disobedient for the next couple of weeks."

"I'm sure you will.. I'm going to shower.. You go get some water and take you medicine.."

"I love you."

"I love you too." I say.

CHAPTER 20

"One more week and I'm all yours baby." Regina whispers in my ear.

"I know baby."

"Mmmm.. Can I taste it?" She smiles at me.

"(Laughs) No.. Because I'm.."

Baby Crying

"And the baby is crying." Regina says. "Again."

"I got her mom." Sam yells.

"Thank you sweetheart." She yells back.

"As I was saying.. I'm headed to work.." I say getting up.

"Are you okay?" She asks.

"Yes.. I'm fine."

"Then why are you avoiding me?" She says as she followed me down stairs.

"I'm not." I say putting on my blazer jacket..

"Bye Emma."

"Regina what's wrong baby?" I ask before I walk out the door because something is bothering her. I look up to see her already up stairs.

"Nothing.. Bye and say hi to your new whore." She yells down stairs and then slams the door.

"Oh hell no." I drop my bag my bag and run up the stairs like my ass was on fire.. "Open the fucking door Regina." I yell as I bang on the door.

"We're leaving mom.. I think we can just walk to school.. Bye we love you guys.." Sam says.

"We love you guys too... And be safe." I yell before they close the door. "Regina open this door or I will kick it down."

"You're going to be late." She says.

"Five seconds.. 5.. 4.... 3... 2.."

"FINE!!! You are so dramatic." She opens the door and walk pass me and go down stairs.

"What did you say."

"I said you were dramatic my love. Kicking down the door??? Really??"

"You said I had a whore." I grab her by the arm and make her look at me. "Don't say that shit Regina.. I'm not cheating on you.. You're making assumptions like you did last time.. I'm not doing this."

"Then don't.." She snatched away from me and went to poor some wine.

"Regina if you.."

Baby Crying...

"Your daughter is crying Emma." She looks at me and drinks her wine.

"What's wrong with you?" I ask.

"You are what's wrong with me... Go get your daughter because all that crying is disturbing my personal peace." She said and I couldn't believe what my ears were hearing.

"Get your act together or so help me god." I walk up stairs and get my daughter.

"(Laughing) I'm going out Emma." Regina yells and the hear the front door.

"Fuck!" I say. "Sorry baby girl.. Don't say bad words okay Abby?" I say and she just looks at me.. "(Laughs) Okay.. Let's get you changed and we will head out."

Sam and Henry School

"Hi I need to check one of my kids out.. I'm.."

"Mom?" I hear Henry say.

"Hey baby.. I was coming to get one of you so you can watch Abby.. I have something to take care of."

"Okay.. Where is ma?"

"Ugh.. She's.. She's okay.. She's coming with me."

"Okay.. We just finished our Exam.. I'll text Sam and tell her we are leaving."

"Thanks kid.. Where do I sign?" I ask the lady at the front desk.

"Here." She points to their names.

"Thank you.. Henry the car is outside.. Come with me while I strap your sister in and you can wait on Sam."

————————————————

"Alright I'll see you three later.. Drive safe." I tell them.

"We will.. Love you mom."

"I love all of you." I close the door and walk over to the car I called for.

"Hey boss." Norman says.

"Thanks for the car."

"You're welcome." I get in the car and drove over to where Regina went.

"Can I help you?" I guy says.

"No you may not." I attempt to walk pass him but of course he is an idiot and got in from of me. "Move.. Or I will arrest you."

"My apologies." He steps aside and let me in. Once I get in I saw Regina at a bar drinking with someone.

"Get up.. Let's go now." I say to her and she laughs.

"(Laughs) I thought you were watching your daughter."

"Our daughter and she is fine.. Thank you for asking."

"Whatever.. I'm busy."

"Regina get up and let's go.." She smiles at me and picks up the shot glass.

"Take another and I swear to god Regina."

"How about you leave the pretty lady alone and get out.. She said she wants to stay." A man says.

"Three things.. One.. Don't tell me what to do when it come to my wife.. Two.. Call my wife pretty again I'll break your face.. Three.. Grab her by the waist again, and I'll arrest you for disturbing my personal peace.. After that, I'll shot you..." I smile at him.. "You got that?"

"I'm so turned on right now." Regina says.

"Get up.. Don't make me carry you out of here."

"Yes Papi." She smiles and run her ass against my front.. "Mmmm.. Don't be jealous, I'll never let that go again." She says. I follow her out and we get in the car.

"What's wrong with you?" I ask.

"Nothing.. Take me home."

"(Laughs) We're not going home."

"Cool.. Then where too?"

"To the hospital."

"For what?!" She yells.

"Because something is wrong with you."

"Yeah.. You're what's wrong with me."

"What did I do??? Huh?? Is it because I haven't fucked you good enough?? Is that?" I yell.

"(Laughs) Keep yelling.. I like it." She says.. What the fuck????

——————

"Get out the car.." I get out and she just looks at me.

"Emma I'm sorry.. Please let's go home." She smiles. And I walk over to the her side of the car.

"Get out of I'll carry you." I say and she again, just looks at me. "Fuck it.." I grab her by the arm and throw her over my shoulder.

"Put me down!" She yells and kicks and slap her ass.. HARD.

"Ooouuuuucchhhh!!" She yells.

"Can I help you?"

"Yes.. I need to see a neurologist, obgyn doctor, and a psychiatrist please."

"Are you okay ma'am?" The lady ask me.

"My wife had a baby a few months ago and she seems to be having a little issues.

"Got it.. Wait here please."

"Fuck you Emma." She yells.

"Yeah.. You'll thank me later."

——————————- Moments Later ————————

"Hi.. I'm Dr. Asher, head of psychology. What can I help you with officer?" He ask.

"My wife had a baby a couple of months ago and now she's been acting like a.."

"A what Emma??? A bitch?" Regina says as she hits me in my back.. (Yes I'm still carrying her)...

"Her words not mine." I say.

"What's going?? Regina, you okay?" Laurel asks.

"Thank god Laurel.. Regina is not like herself." I say.

"Postpartum maybe." She says.

"Can you fix it?" I ask.

"Fix what?" Aaron says.

"Aaron something is wrong with her??? She been bitchy and moody and..."

"Hi Regina." Aaron say.

"Can I go home now?" She asks.

"How about we talk for a minute okay?" Dr. Asher says.

"Fine whatever.. Emma you coming baby?" She asks.

"Ye.. Yeah." I say. And we all walk to the back.

CHAPTER 21

"So what happened?" The doctor ask.

"Emma is mad because I found out about her little whore." Regina says.

"I don't have a whore." I state.

"Well bitch then."

"I'm not cheating on you and the bitch is..."

"Who?? Me?? Go ahead and say it."

"Regina let her speak.. You'll have your turn."

"As I was saying, she's being acting different since we had Abby."

"Postpartum is something very serious." The Obgyn Doctor says.

"How do we fix it? I want my wife back."

"She's talking like I left or something." Regina says.

"You're not the woman I married okay??? You've been acting different and crazy... Abby was crying and you never just let her cry.."

"When did it start?" The neurologist ask.

"About two weeks ago maybe."

"Okay.. Well we can try it with medication and self therapy."

"Wonderful!!!! Can we start today?" I ask.

"Yes. Give us a minute to talk and I'll be right back." They all walk out of the room and leave me and Regina in here.

"So.... You hate me now?" She ask.

"I'll never hate you beautiful." I whisper.

"Sure you do."

"Stop talking Regina."

"(Laughs) Why?? Is the bitch coming out of me?"

"Stop." I whisper.

"You know I understand why you hate me right?"

"I don't hate you."

"(Crying) I don't know why I do the things I do Emma."

"Baby don't cry.. They will fix you, that's why I brought you here."

"Emma I'm.."

"Okay.. Here is some medicine to help with the stress and it is good to be around family as much as possible.. All three doctors said she will be okay." The nurse smiles at me.. And it's the same nurse who was flirting with me when Regina was in labor.

"You keep smiling at my wife like that, they're going to have to prescribe you something 10x stronger than what they gave me." Regina says.

"Sorry.. I'm.. I was just.."

"I know what you were doing but let me be perfectly clear about one thing...." Regina gets up and walk over to her. "She's mine.. Always have been and always will be.. All of you women are obsessed with her because of what she has between her legs but none of you will ever see it... You know why??" Regina asks with a smile.. "My pussy is like a drug to her.. Kind of like how addicts are addicted to drugs.. It's hard to get off of them.. Just like it's hard for Emma to leave me.. So stop smiling at her before I break your face."

"If you're so sure she'll never leave you.. Why do you care if we flirt with her?" The nurse states and I'm scared for her.

"Shit." I whisper.

"You're right." Regina then punches her in the face.

"Baby!" I yell.

"What??? She's a nurse.. I'm sure she can dress her own wound.. Let's go." She grabs my hand and we leave. "You're fucking me tonight." She whispers in my ear when the elevator close. And I didn't do anything but smile at her..

————————————————————

"Ah! Ah! Ahh!!! Fuck yes.. Ah Papi!" She yells.

"(Groans) Damn Gina." I whisper in her ear as I come inside of her.

"You didn't pull out." She says.

"Fuck!" I yell.

"It's okay.. I like having you inside of me."

"(Laughs) Baby."

"Hey.. Thank you for taking me to the hospital.. I don't know what's wrong with me."

"It happens and I've seen what it looks like to not get help so... Just be patient with yourself and let me know if you feel stress."

"Yes Papi." She smiles at me.

"I fucking love you." I say.

"And I love you."

BABY CRYING

"I'll go get Abby.. You go take a cold shower." Regina says.

"Yes ma'am."

————————————————————-

"Did you guys forget we live here too?" Henry asks.

"No.. Why would you ask that kid?" I say.

"Because you too have sex all the time and then when you... Never-mind.. Keep it down or something."

"(Laughs) Sorry baby." Regina says.

"It's not funny mom... I could still hear you with my headphones on." Samantha says.

"Okay.. We are very sorry.. It won't happen again."

"Yeah right." Sam says before her and her brother went out the door.

Knock Knock

"I'll get it." I yell in the kitchen to Regina.

"Okay baby."

"Hi Emma." Beth says.

"Bet.. Beth?? What are you doing here?"

"I wanted to see you."

"Well my wife is here and I can't talk right now."

"Yeah.. Well I need you.. And I need you now."

"I can't just leave and.."

"Emma baby who is at the... Door?" She says when she sees Beth.

"Hi Regina."

"Beth?"

"I need your lovely wife and it's important."

"It always is."

"Unfortunately."

"For how long?" Regina asks.

"A few days.. Maybe a week."

"Okay.. That's fine.. One condition." Regina tells her. "Will you try and fuck my wife again?"

"Ugh.. I.. I'm.. I didn't.. I.. didn't know she told you that."

"Of course she did."

"Right.. I'm sorry about that... And no I will not try and sleep with your wife."

"Good.. Because I can promise you one thing."

"And what's... Whats that Regina??"

"I got her pussy whipped... And she's not going anywhere.." Regina looks at me and kiss me..

"I love you." I whisper.

"I know.. And I love you too.. Now go pack and be careful on your flight to wherever you are going,. call me when your plane lands.. Me and Abby are going to take a nap.."

"Yes ma'am.."

"Hey and go by the school and see Henry and Samantha before you go."

"Will do.." I yell as I jog up the stairs to go pack..

This is going to be a long trip...

CHAPTER 22

A Week Later

"Ma that is not fair." I hear Sam says when I walk in the house.

"What's not fair?" I ask.

"Mom thank god you are back from your trip. Can you please tell Ma that it is not fair that I have to be in the house by 12am."

"12am? I would have said 11pm." I smile at her.

"I should have known you would have been on her side." Sam says.

"Of course.. She is my wife.. Hello beautiful." I walking over to Regina.

"Hey baby.. I missed you." She whispers in my ear.

"And I miss you too." I whisper back and place a kiss on her neck.

"(Moans) Papi." Regina whisper.

"I'm leaving." Sam says.

"(Laughs) Drive safe please." I yell out to Sam. "Where is Abby?" I ask.

"She's with Katherine."

"Oh okay.. I saw Henry leave when I pulled up to the house." I say walking over to the refrigerator to get me a beer.

"You okay?" Regina ask.

"Yeah.. I'm fine baby.. You okay?" I ask.

"I'm fine. You seem different." She says.

FUCK!!!!

"I'm good baby.. Why you say that?"

"Something is off about you." Fuck now what I'm I supposed to do???? Lie??? Yes...

"Nothing is off Gina I told you I'm fine."

"Whatever." She grabs her glass of wine and walks away.

"Regina don't be like that.." I say walking up behind her.

"Like what? Because clearly you are hiding something. Did you sleep with her?" Regina ask.

"(Laughs) Baby.. Come on."

"Well you didn't deny it."

"For fuck sakes Regina no I did not sleep with her or anybody else late for that matter.."

"Well did you kiss her or.."

"Regina I didn't fuck nobody or kiss anyone... To clear that up, No I did not cheat on you.. Thanks for trusting me by the way." I grab my coat and walk towards the door.

"And where are you going?" She ask.

"To get some air because clearly I am the bad guy right now."

"Emma I'm sorry.. Please don't leave." She grabs my hand and pulls me away from the door.

"I didn't cheat on you Regina." I say looking at her.

"Okay.. I believe you, but Emma you are hiding something."

"Yes but fucking somebody is not it.. Damn Regina." I yell.

"Then what is it?"

"I got a promotion." I say,

"And why is that so hard for you to tell me?"

"Because it's in Spain and I will be gone for 18 months."

"Excuse me?"

"Yeah.. That's why I didn't say anything."

"So what? You were just going to leave and not say anything?"

"Yeah Regina. I was going to leave my wife and three kids behind while I go catch bad guys." I say walking away.

"Emma stop.."

"Come on Regina, you know damn well I wasn't going to leave you guys.. I was waiting on them to call me back so I could decline the offer, but here you go Assuming shit as always." I say as I'm walking up stairs and she's following me.

"Emma I'm sorry."

"Okay."

"Where.. Where are you going?"

"To take a shower?"

"Why.. Are doing all of this stuff right now.. Let's talk first and.."

"Oh my god Regina.. I'm not taking a shower because I was cheating on you., Okay?? I didn't cheat.. I just want to take a shower.. It's been a long day and I want to take a shower.. You can join me if you want, but please drop the cheating bullshit.. You should know by now that you're all I want and need."

"I better be."

"I mean look at you.. And let's not forget about that ass of yours.. Man do I miss watching it as I fuck you from behind."

"I tell you what?? After you decline that offer, how about you join me in the pool?"

"At this hour?" I ask.

"Unless you have better things to do."

"No ma'am."

"See you later Papi." She whispers in ear before she licks it.

"'Mmmmmm.. I can't wait." She turns to walk away and before she gets to far I smack her ass..

"Ahh!!!! Fuck Papi.. Wait till later." She closes the bedroom door and I go take a shower..

——————————————————————————————————————

—-

"Mom can you please tell Sam to stay out of my business?" Henry ask.

"Okay but Henry, go back inside okay."

"What's wrong with you?" He ask.. And I am not about to tell my son that his mother is giving me head underneath the water in this pool.

"Nothing.."

"Fine.. Where is Ma?"

"In the kitchen.. Ugh.. Yeah.. She's getting more wine."

"Oh.. Okay.. Tell her I'm back from the game."

"Will do son.." He walks away and once I here the door close, I lost it.. I couldn't hold it in anymore. "Ah!!! Fuck!!!!!!" I yelled. And she came from underneath the water. "Fuck Regina."

"About time.. What took you so long to come?"

"Your son came down here."

"Shut up!? No he didn't."

"Oh yes he did."

"Perfect timing with them."

"Of course.. Now.. Are you going to feed me." I ask her.

"Take me." She whispers.

I stick my fingers in her mouth and told her to wet them for me. "That's so hot." I whisper. I take them out of her mouth and put my hand inside of her bikini bottoms.. She's so fucking wet.. I rub her clit a few times before I stick my fingers inside of her begging hole.

"(Gasps) Em-ma baby.."

"Mmmm.. Put one of your legs around my waist." I say and she doesn't hesitate to do so.. Once she do that I pump my fingers fast and hard..

"Oh my god." Her eyes roll to the back of her head and her mouth is wide open.

"Your so fucking beautiful." I say and she smiles at me.. "I love the way you look at me when your coming." As her eyes roll to the back of her head this time I take my fingers out of her and replace them with my dick.

"(Passionate Screams) Ah!!"

"Put your arms around me and hold on tight." I whisper in her ear.. "I'm going to fuck you now."

CHAPTER 23

"How was your trip?" One of my Officers ask me.

"It was okay.. Long, but it was okay."

"Did she try and get into your pants again?"

"No.. No but she did say she couldn't believe I told Regina about it."

"I bet.."

"Your cousin is crazy..' I laugh.

"I know it."

"Hi there.. Now what is a pretty little thing like you doing here all by yourself?" I hear officer Cameron Briggs say. He's one of my new recruits.

"I'm looking for Emma." I hear my name and that's when I know it's Regina.

"Boss lady is busy with paper work how about I help you.. I'm sure I could be of assistance." He says with a smile.

"I bet you could be but I want Emma.. And thank you for the help." She says and makes her way over to me but he grabs her by the arm, not to hard though because if he did I'll shoot his ass.. Literally.. I will shoot him..

"I'm sure I could help you ma'am.. I'm sorry I didn't get your name."

"That's because I didn't give it to you."

"My name is Cameron Briggs." He says with a smile.

"And my name is Regina."

"Nice to meet you Regina, it would go good with Briggs one day."

"Sorry.. I have a last name already and I like it more the way it is.. I would like my arm back please."

"So you're not going to tell me what your last name is??" He says.

"Oh shit.. I'm sorry.. Baby do you want to tell him what my last name is or should I do it?" She says looking at me, which causes him to look at me.

"Baby?? Wait a second sooooo.. You and Emma are.."

"Married?? Yes.. My name is Regina Swan-Mills.. And I'm Emma's Wife and the mother of our 3 children." Regina smiles.

"Boss I'm sorry I didn't know.. Had I known she was your wife I wouldn't have crossed that line."

"You're new.. You'll learn." I say..

"My arm?" Regina repeats..

"Shit.. Sorry.. My apologies.." He let's go and Regina walks over to me with a smirk on her face..

"Hey baby." She says and I grab her by the waist and kiss her..

"Hello beautiful."

"Can you have lunch with me." She says.

"I can't leave but you are welcome to stay.."

"Okay.. I'll meet you in your office in about 30 minutes.. I'll go grab us something." She winks at me and walks off and that's when I noticed Officer Briggs staring at her.

"Is my wife going to be a problem for you???? I would hate to have to fire you before your shift even gets interesting."

"(Clears Throat) No ma'am.. I'm sorry."

"Apologizing will not help you but I do except it.. Now get to work.."
I walk off and go to my office and shut the door..... Fucking great.. I
hate when people go after my wife.... She's mine.. And mine alone..

————————————————————————————

"Did you apply to any colleges yet?" I ask Sam.

"No not yet.. I'm waiting another 6 months to a year." She says..

"I'm Sorry.. What?????"

"Ma said I could." She says..

"Baby??" I call for Regina.

"Yes my love?" She walks in the living to join us.

"Sam said she was waiting an awful long time to go to college."

"Yeah she wants to work a year and then go off to college.. She is
graduating early after all.."

"Why didn't you tell me?" I ask Sam.

"I didn't think you would approve. That's why I'm hear tonight
instead of out with my friends.. I only told ma this morning so don't
think we we're keeping this from you.. We would never talk about
stuff behind your back mom."

"(Laughs) I know that baby.. Thank you."

"I love you mom and I promise I'm going to college. I just want to work first and.."

"I'm not trying to cut you off or anything but why do you want to work? You have a trust fund with half a million dollars in it and you also have another account with $400,000 dollars in it... Let's not forget the half million is yours to spend sand 400,000 is for college."

"I know that mom, but me and Henry already get teased enough about how we don't understand what's it like to come from nothing.. They always say we don't know the struggle."

"Well that may be true but me and your mother did struggle.. For a long time and that's why we worked our ass off so that you, your brother and your sister don't have to."

"I know and I love you both for that, but I still want to do it.. I promise I'm not going to work anywhere dangerous."

"I know.. So come work for me."

"I'm sorry?" She says.

"All you have to do is make sure all the paper is in the correct order and then take them to your mother's office."

"That's it?"

"That's it.. And I promise you will clock in like the rest of us and get paid with a real check.. I will try and pay you out of my pocket."

"Thank you mom... I would love too."

"You would love to what?" Henry ask.

"Mom said I can come work with her when we graduate.."

"Oh okay.." Henry says and he gives a small smile but it's a sad one.

"Hey buddy what's wrong?"

"It's nothing.. I'm going to my room."

"Henry Swan-Mills you come back here." Regina says. Henry looks at her and then comes to sit. "What's wrong baby?"

"It's nothing really."

"I guess we'll all sit here until you tell us.. Here, hold your sister I have to pee." Regina hand Abby to Henry and she starts to smile..

"Hey baby girl?" Henry whispers to her with a smile.

"Henry? Look at me." I say.

"Mom I'm fine."

"Your sister is not applying to be a cop if that's why you're upset."

"Fucking great!!!" He yells.

"HENRY!!!" Regina yells at him.

"Sorry ma.. I got a little excited.. I thought my sister was applying to be a cop."

"Well she's not.. She will be doing paper work."

"Okay.. So does that mean I can apply to be a cop?"

"No." I say.

"But mom I want to.. I see what you do and I want to help people and.."

"There are other ways to help people.. Become a doctor."

"I want to be a cop like you." He says.

"No.. And this conversation is over.. I'll take your sister upstairs and put her to bed." I say getting up and reaching for Abby..

"Mom I.." He started to say something and I just keep walking.. I will not have my son follow into my foot steps and get hurt.. Our family had already been through enough.

"Emma?" I hear Regina say.

"The answer is no Regina.. I'm going to put Abby down for bed and then I'll join you in our room okay?" I say and she nods before I shut the door to Abby's room..

CHapter 24

"**Y**ou completely cut him off without giving him a chance to explain himself." Regina said when I walked in the room.

"I heard him and the answer is no."

"He already applied, but I haven't put the transfer in yet."

"He did what?"

"I didn't know.. I only found out 30 minutes ago.. I looked through my emails and he put it in Friday."

"No Regina.. That's my final answer." I say walking to the bathroom.

"September 28th 2001... Is that what this is about?"

"I'm not doing this." I say.

"Doing what??? Talking??? What happened to you was awful and terrifying but that doesn't mean it will happen to him."

"So you can see the future now?"

"Don't be an asshole Emma." Regina yells.

"Wake up Abby will you." I say when she yells.

"Emma you have to let him grow up. Your dad didn't want you following in his footsteps and what did you do??? You did it anyway."

"WHICH IS WHY I DON'T WANT THE SAME THING FOR MY SON!" I yell and she gets up and leave the room. FUCK!!!! "Regina baby I'm sorry." I say walking behind her.

"I'm sleeping on the couch tonight.." She says.

"Mom.. I'm sorry if I made you upset." Henry say and when I look at him I can tell he has been crying.

"Henry it's not your fault.. It's mine.."

"Mom are okay?" Sam asks.

"I'm fine.. I just.." I couldn't talk because when I looked at Regina she was crying.. I shouldn't have yelled at her.. I forgot what happened last time I got anger.. "Regina I.."

(Baby Crying)

"I'll go get her." I say walking off.

"NO!" Regina yells.. "I got her, maybe you should lay down."

"I'll go with ma." Sam says.

"Okay." I say sadly.

"Mom.. Maybe you should lay down and we can talk tomorrow." Henry says before he walks upstairs.

Great.... Now my family is afraid of me again.. Fucking great.... Maybe I should leave..

When I notice they are asleep in Abby's room, I pack a few bags and leave.. I wrote a note and said I'm sorry and that I love them..

4am (3 hours away from home)

"Can I get room please?" I ask the lady at the front desk.

"Sure.. How many nights?" She asks.

"A month for now."

"Oh wow.. Are you here visiting or something."

"Yeah, or something." I say and she hands me a key.. "Thank You."

"You're welcome gorgeous. And if you need anything.. And I mean anything.. Please page the front desk.." She say's smiling..

"I'm good.. But thanks, and no room service please.."

"You got it." I walk out the door and drive around to the back.. I'm glad they had rooms available in the back.. I want to hide my car..

———8am ———

Ring Ring Ring Ring

"Fuck..." I say waking up to my phone ringing. I didn't even look at it, I just answered. "Hello." I say dryly.

"Emma.. Where are you? I'm coming." Regina says.

"(Sighs) Regina.. I'm.."

"Tell me where you are?" She cuts me off..

"Just know I'm safe.. I have to go.. Tell the kids I said I love them and kiss baby girl for me.. I love you Regina.. I love you so much baby.. Bye." And with that I hung up the phone..

Knock Knock.....

"I said no room service and..." I open the door to see Henry and Sam standing there.. "what are you doing here and how did you find me?" I ask. "Come in.." I grab them both and pull ten in because it was cold as shit outside..

"We tracked your phone when you left late last night.. I saw your note and didn't want you to do anything crazy like... You know like last time.." Henry says.

"I'm sorry if I scared you guys... How is ugh.. How is your mama doing?"

"Please don't get mad." Sam whispers.

"I promise." I say looking her in the eyes..

"Mom thinks were at school."

"Excuse me?" I ask.

"She didn't hear us leave this morning and I made look as if we made coffee and left for school." Henry says.

"Call her and tell her where you are right now please." I tell Sam. She pulls out her phone and calls her mama.

"Sam baby I can't talk right now I'm trying to get ahold of your mom and she's not answering."

"Regina I'm okay."

"Emma??? Wait where are you and Sam why aren't you in school.. Hello Henry I know you're there too."

"Sorry mama.."

"Where are you?" Regina ask. And they both look at me..

"I'm three hours away from home.. I'm at a hotel about a mile away from the highway.." I say..

"Estás en tantos problemas cuando llego allí." And with that she hangs up the phone..

"Great.. She's going to kill all of us."

"I think she said we are in trouble."

"Are you two hungry?" I ask.

"Starving.." Henry say.

"Let's go get breakfast before your mama gets here." I go in the bathroom and put on some clothes.. It's been about 2 hours and a few minutes or so since the kids got here because they wanted to take a nap before we go because they've been driving all day.. When I came out there was a knock at the door.

"I'm coming." I yell.. Sam and Henry was laying across the bed.

"Mama didn't make it that fast." Sam said.

"(Laughs) No she didn't..." I opened the door and it's the lady from last night. Shit!!

"Good morning.. I was hoping you was up.." She says smiling..

"I'm headed to breakfast with my kids."

"Oh you have kids?" She ask.

"And a wife.. And another baby at home." Sam says.

"Right ugh.. You'll be here tonight though right?"

"No.. She'll need that refund by the way." Henry said with his arms folded.

"You just got here and you're leaving.. I was hoping to see you tonight." She said smiling at me.. Looking me up down, yeah she is flirting....

"I can't.. I'm with my family and I.."

"How about you call me tonight when you're alone." She comes closer to my body and puts her number in my back pocket.

"I'm married and I'm.." I try to speak but she puts her finger to my lips.

"I didn't ask you if you were married.. And what is that?" She asks looking down at me and that's when I noticed she felt me.. She reach for my belt and grab her hands.. This lady is bold.. My teenage kids are here and she's just going for it... Wow..

"Hey.. Hey.. Hey... Stop.. Don't do that.. I told you I was married."

"I said call me, not tell me your life story."

"And I said you better back the fuck up before I beat your ass." I look up to see Regina standing there in her pants suit and high heels on.. I have a beautiful ass wife...

"And you are?" The girl ask.

"Her wife.. So can you kindly go do your job and stop harassing my wife.. That's all mine." Regina says and the girl smiles at her.. "Yeah, and when I say all of it is mine... I'm talking about that too." She points to the front of my pants before she looks at me..

"Call me." She whispers to me before she turns around a leave.

"That bitch better find her something safe to do because she is zero seconds from getting her ass kicked." Regina says.

"Hey beautiful." I say with a smile.

"Hey baby and you're in so much trouble." She whispers in my ear when she gives me a hug.

"I sure hope so." I whisper back.

"Ewww." Sam says.

"You two should be in school.. This will not go unpunished.."

"Yes ma'am." Henry says.

"Here.. Go by something eat and bring us something back.. I also want coffee.. I'm going to stay here and talk to your mom." Regina says handing Sam her card.

"Oh god... You're not going to have sex are you?" Sam says.

"I don't know.. Should we?" Regina says with a smile.. "Maybe I should let that bitch know where she stands." She looks me up and down and walks over to me.. "Go eat you guys and don't forget my coffee." Regina says walking past me and the kids say bye and walk off really fast... I walk in the room and shut the door.....

"Regina I.." I start to talk but she stops me....

"Take off your pants." She says.

"(Laughs) What??? You can't be serious?" I ask..

"I'm so serious.." She says talking off her clothes. "You're going to fuck me and I'm going to let that bitch know who's pussy owns you." She says and I stand there looking at my wife because I don't know what to do.. Do I fuck her or tell her she has nothing to prove, because I have zero interest in that woman.. ZERO!!! How could I when I had Regina..

"Baby you don't have to prove anything to her and I'm.." Before I could finish, she was on her knees in front of me.. "Fuck." This is happening...

CHAPTER 25

"(Moans) Oh god.. Yes, don't stop Emma." She moans loudly.

"Fuck Regina.. I'm gonna cum." I say looking at her.

"Cum with me." She say against my lips. "(Moans) You're so fucking deep inside of me."

"(Moans) You feel so good Regina... I love you.. Fuck!!!! I'm coming." I say going faster. Seconds later Regina back arched and she screamed..

"Ah!!! Fuck!!" She pants..

"That was amazing." I say rolling off her.

"It was.." She gets up and grab her phone.

"What are you doing?" I ask.

"Calling to check on our baby.. She was sleep when I left.. Katherine said she would call when she wakes up."

"Could you put some clothes on please?" I ask.

"Why?? Am I distracting you?" She smirks.

"Yes you are and it's not helping." I look down and see that I have another boner...

"Give me a second and I'll suck you off." She says putting her phone down after texting.. "Now where were we?" She climbs on top of me and strokes my length.

"Mmmmmm... Fuck!! I'm good baby.. It will go away."

"Shut up and enjoy it." And with that she took me in her mouth.

"Fuck.. Yes baby.. I love you.. I fucking love you.. (Moans)... Ahhhh... Yes.." I grab hair and move it out of her face so I could see her and what a sight it was.. "My god your beautiful." I whisper.

Knock Knock!!!!!

"Oh shit." I say and Regina doesn't care she keeps going. "Uhhh.. I'm busy.. Come back later." I managed to say..

"It's time to go.. I'm tired." Sam yells.

"Okay.. Hold.. (Moans) Fuck.. Hold on.." I grab Regina hair and hold her in place while I fuck her mouth. "Ahhh.. Just like that baby.. Take it.. Ahhh... Fuck!!!! I'm gonna cum.. Fuck... I'm coming.. I'm coming.. I'm coming.. Ahh.. Ahhhhh." When I come I push my length further in her mouth so she could swallow me down.. "I'm sorry.. I didn't mean to get so rough I just.."

"I liked it.. No need to apologize.. You haven't fucked my mouth in a long time.." She smiles..

"I'm aware.."

"Moms!!!!" Sam yells..

"Okay I'm coming." Regina gets up and open the door.

"Jesus ma.. Fix your hair and your lip stick.. I can't even look at you." Sam says..

"Don't look at me like that." Regina says..

"I'm waiting in the car." She says.

"Me too." Henry says and Regina closes the door...

"I'm sorry." I say.

"What?"

"I'm sorry.. For snapping.. I didn't mean too I just.. I.."

"Emma you don't have to explain anything to me.. Never.. Now put on some clothes before I decide to fuck you again." She smiles..

"Yes ma'am.."

Home.......

"Home sweet home.. Can I see my baby girl?" I ask Regina..

"Of course." We walk upstairs and there is Katherine holding my baby girl in her arms asleep..

"She is going to be spoiled and don't think I'm going to hold her all night... Wake her up." I say.

"No.. She just laid down." Katherine says..

"Your spoiling her." I say..

"Yes I am.."

"Regina.. Babe.." I say looking at Regina and she is smiling.

"Don't look at her." Katherine steps to my face. "Just because you know how to fuck her good, doesn't mean she is going to take your side all the time. I've known her longer than you."

"(Laughs) Give me my daughter please." I ask.

"Here and don't wake her up." She says.

"Yes mom." I say in a little kids voice.

"Ha ha ha.. Very funny.. Regina come have a drink with me." She grab Regina and walk out the room.

"It's only 4pm." I say.

"We know mom." Katherine yells back. And I later hear her laugh.

"Okay.. Yeah, I don't like her very much princess." I say to Abby.

Dinner

"How are you feeling mom?" Samantha asks.

"I'm fine sweetheart... Thank you." I say smiling.

"That's good.. I'm glad you're feeling better." Henry says.

"Thank you kid.. I'm just glad I have a family like you guys.. (sniffs) One who loves me even when I'm stupid." I say getting up from the table.. "You all finish eating.. I'm going to get some sleep.. Clean up for your ma when you get done eating.. Good night.. I love y'all."

"Emma wait.." Regina says.

"I'm fine baby." I lean in and kiss her. "I love you so much."

"I love you too.. Please finish eating."

"I ate most of it.. I can't eat much when I take that medicine.. I'll have to eat more in the morning for breakfast."

"You sure you're okay." Regina ask.

"Yes mom." I say reminding Regina about her and Kathrine laughing earlier tonight about calling me mom.

"Ewwww." Sam says. "Yeah.. She is definitely okay.." She says looking at her brother..

"Goodnight.." I say walking over giving Abby a kiss. "Sam when you guys get done cleaning the kitchen.. Put your sister to sleep please."

"Okay mom.. I love you.. Goodnight."

"I love y'all too.. Goodnight Sam.. Goodnight Henry and Regina my love, I will see you upstairs when you come to bed." I say walking out the kitchen. What a long night this is going to be....

CHAPTER 26

"Emma it is so good to see you. I really wish it was under different circumstances." My therapist said.

"Me too and thank you for seeing me so soon."

"Anytime Emma. So what happened?"

"I yelled at Regina and."

"Emma.. Did you hurt your family?"

"No.. I didn't mean to yell it just happened and I ran as fast as I could.. I promise I wasn't going to get angry like last time.. I swear."

"Okay.. So what happened?"

"Henry wants to become a cop and I don't want that for him.."

"I can see why that made you upset."

"Yes and when I yelled Regina stormed off and.."

RING RING !!!!!!!

"It's Regina.. She's calling me."

"Do you wish to answer?" She asks.

"No.. I want to finish talking."

"Okay.. Please continue."

"Yes so she stormed off.. Her and the twins went to sleep in baby girls room so I packed a bag and left.. I wrote a note and told them I loved them but my cleaver twins traced my cell phone and found me.. Regina showed up hours later and convinced me to come back home." I say smiling.

"That's good.. I'm happy she came around really quickly."

"When I got angry and threw that vase, I never intended for it to hit Regina and then I started breaking stuff and yelling.. My kids didn't talk to me for almost two months and Regina didn't even feel safe being in the house with me by herself."

"And how does that make you feel?? Knowing that your family fear you?"

"Bad.. I feel like shit and that's why I tried to leave."

"Emma.. Do you believe you will hurt your family again?"

"No.. Like I said it was just a bad argument and I didn't mean to yell that loud.. I'm sorry if I want a better life for my son."

"I understand Emma.. Just try talking to Regina and see what she says."

"I will.. She's called me like 10 times already."

"You should go home and talk to her.. My phone is always available to you and your family."

"Thank you Dr. Robin."

"You're welcome and tell everyone I said hello and I will be looking forward to meeting the new member of the family."

"Yes. I will let Regina know we need to schedule a dinner with you."

"I would love that." I reach over and give her a hug.

"You have a good night Emma."

"You too Dr. Robin." And with that I left..

Home ....

"Emma I swear to god if you do that again I will kill you." Regina say when I walk in the house.

"What did I do?"

"Why didn't you answer your phone?" She ask.

"Ma.. I found moms location and it said she was at Jessie's office and.." Sam stops talking when she sees me standing there.. "Oh.. Hey Mom."

"Hey Sam." I smile at her.

"You went to see Jessie?" Regina ask.

"Yes.. I needed to talk to her and she was able to see me today."

"Right.... Samantha baby.. Grab Abby and take her to your friend house and tell your brother to grab some dinner."

"That's code for you two are going to have sex isn't??? You too need help."

"Or maybe you should stay out of your parents business." Regina says.

"You don't have to tell me twice. Come on Abby." Samantha grab Abby and leaves out the door.

"So?" I say.

"You went to see Jessie and didn't tell me?" Regina asks.

"Baby I'm fine.. I just told her what happened and we talked about it. She said we need to have her over for dinner."

"That would be nice. Tell her tomorrow night at 6pm." Regina says walking away.

"Yes ma'am,"

"And Emma?" Regina says.

"Yeah Baby?" I ask looking at her.

"Next time you need to see your therapist, you tell me."

"I will baby.. I promise."

"You better." She says and she goes into the bathroom and closes the door.

"I love it when you talk dirty to me." I yell.

"If you didn't stress me out so much maybe I could do more than talk dirty to you."

"Mmmm.. Please tell me more."

"Go pick up baby girl from Katherine's house please." Regina says as she walks out the bathroom in nothing but a thong.

"You're evil."

"Oh yeah." She walks up to me and sits on my lap facing me. "Touch me here." She grabbed both of my hands and made me squeeze her boobs.

"(Moans) Fuck!"

"Now be a good wife and get Abby please." And with that she disappeared into the closet.

"And Emma baby?"

"Yes ma'am."

"Take care of that before you go." She says pointing to my pants.

"You caused it." I say walking over to her. "Maybe you should take care of it." Pushing her against wall was something that she loved the most.

"I don't think so."

"Then I'll be going outside like this." I walk away from her and grab my jacket.

"Emma?" She calls my name and I ignore her as I continue to walk down stairs and out the door. "EMMA!" She yells and I get in my car and pull off.

———————

"Hey Kate. I'm here to pick up Abby." As I'm pulling up I see her and Abby walking from the mail box.

"Hey.... Sam just dropped her off like 20 minutes ago. She's next door at Becky's house."

"We figured she would drop her off over here when she got to Becky's house."

"Right... I will go get her bag. Hold her right quick."

"I can't get out the car Kate. Your best friend is one evil woman."

"No way.. are you... (laughs) I'm sorry it's not funny.. I'll put her the car seat for you and tell Regina to come out and get her out for you."

"That would be great.. Thanks."

————

"Emma are you fucking serious?" Regina ask.

"Am I serious??? Are you serious??"

"You went out looking like that and I..."

(Ring Ring)

"Hello?" Regina answers the phone. "Yea she's here. Sam and Henry came out to get Abby Emma won't get out the car. Kate that was not my fault she is the one who.... Wait who side are you on???? You're my friend??? (Laughs) I know right.. Yeah I thought so... Yeah I should do that to her shouldn't I??"

"I'm sorry??? Do what exactly?" I ask and all Regina do is smile.

"I'll call you later Kate." She hands up the phone and get in the car. "Drive around back and park the car."

"Why??" I ask.

"Unless you want me to fuck your brains out right here??? I mean I would love for the entire neighborhood to hear how quick I can make you feel weak."

"You wouldn't?" I say and she climbs over in the driver seat and straddle my legs.

"I'm going to drive you insane." She says grinding on me. "You make me so wet. All these years we've been together and yet you still make me run like a River." She leans up and line herself up with me before she slowly sit back down. "(Gasps) Oh god."

"Mmmm... So fucking tight." I whisper in her ear.

"I could come like this... I'm getting to old for this shit.. I come too fast."

"Don't ever feel bad about how quickly you come.. And you're still beautiful." I say moving her hips back and forth.

"(Moans) Shit Emma.. Suck on my nipples and look at me at the same time." She says and who am I to deny her that. "Yes baby... Just like that. You're going to make me come like that."

"I intend to." I say holding her in place as I thrust deep inside of her. "(Moans) So fucking sexy.... Damn woman.."

"(Moans) I'm coming Emma.. I'm coming I'm coming I'm coming!!!! AH!!! Ahhhhhh!!!" She yells and that's when I know she got EXACTLY what she needed.

"I could watch you come all day." I say kissing her lips.

"You're carrying me in the house because my legs no longer work."

"I'll be happy too." I smile at her.